the

HOMESCHOOL
LIBERATION
LEAGUE

the

HOMESCHOOL LIBERATION LEAGUE

lucy frank

Dial Books for Young Readers

DIAL BOOKS FOR YOUNG READERS
A division of Penguin Young Readers Group
Published by The Penguin Group • Penguin Group (USA) Inc., 375 Hudson Street, New York,
NY 10014, U.S.A. • Penguin Group (Canada), 90 Eglinton Avenue East, Suite 700, Toronto,
Ontario, Canada M4P 2Y3 (a division of Pearson Penguin Canada Inc.) • Penguin Books Ltd,
80 Strand, London WC2R 0RL, England • Penguin Ireland, 25 St. Stephen's Green, Dublin 2,
Ireland (a division of Penguin Books Ltd) • Penguin Group (Australia), 250 Camberwell Road,
Camberwell, Victoria 3124, Australia (a division of Pearson Australia Group Pty Ltd) • Penguin
Books India Pvt Ltd, 11 Community Centre, Panchsheel Park, New Delhi - 110 017, India •
Penguin Group (NZ), 67 Apollo Drive, Rosedale, North Shore 0632, New Zealand (a division
of Pearson New Zealand Ltd) • Penguin Books (South Africa) (Pty) Ltd, 24 Sturdee Avenue,
Rosebank, Johannesburg 2196, South Africa • Penguin Books Ltd, Registered Offices: 80 Strand,
London WC2R 0RL, England

Title page photo © 2009 by Veer
Designed by Teresa Dikun
Text set in Adobe Caslon
Printed in the U.S.A.
10 9 8 7 6 5 4 3 2 1

Library of Congress Cataloging-in-Publication Data
Frank, Lucy.
The Homeschool Liberation League / Lucy Frank.
    p. cm.
Summary: Thirteen-year-old Katya convinces her parents to try homeschooling her for a month,
but while she is finally excited about learning—and about Milo, the violin prodigy who lives
nearby—not everything works out as she had hoped.
ISBN 978-0-8037-3230-8
[1. Homeschooling—Fiction. 2. Middle schools—Fiction. 3. Schools—Fiction.
4. Gifted children—Fiction. 5. Individuality—Fiction. 6. Violinists—Fiction.
7. Family life—Connecticut—Fiction. 8. Connecticut—Fiction.] I. Title.
PZ7.F8515Hom 2009   [Fic]—dc22   2008023922

*

for Marion
and in memory of Irwin

*

CHAPTER

1

The first day of eighth grade,
I took the bus to school, walked
through the door, turned around,
and went home.

2

My braid thumped my backpack and my backpack joggled against my back as I raced down the hill at the edge of town. I stayed off Route 20, where Dad might spot me on his way to work, or Mom, or Grandpa, coming home from breakfast at the Dutch Treat. The road was already giving off that tarry smell. School would be an oven. I'd never know. My friends thought I'd lost my mind. I didn't care. Even the goldenrod in the ditch, which I'd always hated because it meant the end of summer, suddenly looked beautiful to me. What was it Dimitri had called goldenrod at camp? Something magical-sounding.

"We know, you loved it, you were inspired, you had a crush on the nature counselor, who loved your mind and called you Katya." I could still hear Lindsey popping her gum on the bus this morning. "It was camp. Everyone loves camp. You're not supposed to love school. You just do it." She wiped off the eyeliner she'd messed up when the bus took a corner and drew on a new line. "So can we move on, please?"

"To Tyler, maybe?" Jessie said. "Remember, Tyler loves your mind."

"Uh . . ." Lindsey raised her eyebrow. "Mind?"

Alyssa touched my shoulder. "It's okay, Kaity. If you seriously don't want to be with him, you'll just walk over, give him the hat—"

"No, she won't!" Jessie looked horrified. "She spent all last year trying to get him! Oooh! Linds, don't look now! Josh is staring at you!"

They'd been my friends since preschool: Jessie, with her black-jelly-bean eyes and brace-y grin, and hair that even my mom's strongest hair tamer couldn't tame; Alyssa, shaped all wrong to be cool, but still trying; and sometimes-really-nice Lindsey.

"Ooh, hey, Kaity." Jessie tapped my arm as we passed the school secretary's house. "Think Pinchbeck's retired yet?"

"Or died?" Lindsey picked up on it.

"In Westenburg's arms!" Jessie puffed out her cheeks, tucked her chin, and began reciting my last year's claim to fame: "*The Toes Knows, or The Secret Life of Harold Westenburg*. I may look like your basic elderly, bald principal. But I have a dark secret. I was born with twelve toes. Six on each foot. And they're not small. Ever since I was a little tyke my mother has had to knit me special—'"

"Stop!" I put my hands over my ears. I'd only written the stupid thing to keep from falling asleep during assembly, but then I'd passed it to Jess, who passed it down the row, and yes, they thought it was the greatest thing since the

Gettysburg Address, but why I didn't stop her, and why I kept on doing things like that . . .

"We're just trying to cheer you up," Alyssa said.

"By reminding me what a jerk I was?"

"It was funny!"

"I know," I said. And Jessie did a great Westenburg. "But . . ."

"'So what, you say?'" Jessie went on reciting. "'Unless you go barefoot, nobody will know. Well, I can no longer live a lie. I must marry Ms. Pinchbeck, who I've been having a passionate affair with for twenty years, and finally take my socks off when we have marital relations.'" She switched to an old-lady voice. "'Dearest Harold, I don't care if you have twelve toes on each foot! I have a little secret too, darling. That hair you love to run your fingers through? I hang it in the closet every night. Yours till death do us part, Aida Pinchbeck.'"

"And remember Valentine's Day, when Danny read it over the PA?" Lindsey said. "That was soooo hilarious! And your Roy drawing, Kaity? What do you think? Think Mr. Z. had Roy removed?"

"Oh no!" Jessie cried. "Then what'll happen to Roy's little cap?"

Roy being our last year's English teacher's wart—a wart so big, it stuck up through his hair. I was the one who'd named it. I'd also told everyone it could pick up signals from space and that we should knit a cap for it. I couldn't believe I'd been so mean. I liked Mr. Zingarelli. He was the best teacher in the school. And one of the few who liked me. I wished I was back home, under the covers.

No, I didn't. I wanted to be in my tent again, at camp, with Rosie, reading. Or doing a butterfly count with my counselor Dimitri, listening to him call out: "Great spangled fritillary! Silvery checkerspot!" in his crazy Russian accent. At camp there was no need for me to start trouble. At camp I didn't worry if I was good enough or too good, not perfect enough or too perfect for anyone to like me. At camp even my name was different.

"I didn't have a crush on Dimitri," I said. "And I never said he loved my mind."

I had "an interesting mind," is what he'd said. And that he loved my discovery journal, and that I had to keep writing in it when I got home. Which, of course, I hadn't.

But if I did . . . I could already see myself sending it to him at grad school, and him sending it back with notes like: "Katya, this is brilliant."

"Yo! Earth to Kaity. We're here! And there's Tyler." Lindsey handed me her lip gloss.

"You don't have to say anything," Alyssa whispered as we got off the bus. "If you give him his hat, he'll get it. He'll know you're dumping him."

I couldn't. And not because he looked so cute and hot slouched against the wall with his friends that it was easy to forget that he was as interesting as a crash dummy. Or that I was thinking, Who am I to dump the hottest guy in school? Which, in spite of everything, I was. It was more like when your mom brings out the naked baby pictures and your insides squirm, and you're like, *No! Do not make me look at that! I was never like that! I did not sleep with Tyler's hat under my pillow! That could not have been me!*

Meanwhile my friends, having given up on me, were waving eagerly to Francesca Halloran, perkily preppy and popular and perfect as ever as she crossed the yard surrounded by her girls. The old me didn't just ache to be Francesca's friend. I wanted to be her. Even last year, when I was working so hard to be the anti-Francesca, I was still jealous of her.

"Guess how much her jeans cost?" Alyssa said.

"I know!" Jessie nodded. "A hundred seventy dollars!"

"Not that much. A hundred and seven. And see that skirt Rachel has on?" Alyssa pointed to one of Francesca's entourage. "I almost bought it, but it made my legs look fat."

"Well, check out *her* legs," I said. "And what did she do to her hair? She looks like a tangerine."

And why was I being mean about Rachel? I liked Rachel.

The bell clanged.

"Kaity," Lindsey said, "you're blocking traffic. Everyone's looking at us. And not in a good way. Come on."

That horribly familiar numbness was coming over me. If it's possible to be numb and lonely at the same time. I felt like I might gag, or faint.

"Kaity, would you please stop looking like you're about to die," Alyssa said as everyone started swarming toward the doors. She took my arm and led me through. "You'll be fine. By the end of homeroom, you'll be used to it again."

"I'm going home," I said.

Compared to the pack at camp, this one felt light as a marshmallow. Which could have been because it was empty, except for the hat, my notebook, lunch, and the change of top I couldn't stop myself from throwing in, in case the one I'd picked out for The First Day of School turned out to be all wrong. But there'd be no wrong, now or ever again. I felt like I could run forever.

As I cut into the woods behind the golf course, I composed my letter to the principal. *Dear Mr. Westenburg, I am hereby withdrawing from Martin Van Buren Middle School. As you must know, I was not happy*—Uh-uh. Too bland—*totally miserable*—too whiny—*I am finding school stupefying.* Points for vocabulary there! *Don't blame my mom and dad for not answering those letters you sent home. I wanted them to hear the truth from my own lips.* That hadn't exactly happened yet, but now it could. *You should also know, Mr. Westenburg, that I learned more in a month at Wilderness Discovery Camp than I learned in seven years at school.*

I was deep enough in the woods now to stop running, so I sat down on a fallen tree to catch my breath, and, since lunch period meant nothing to me anymore, eat lunch. Eew. Tuna with chipotle mayo. Mom must have gotten that off the Food Network.

Mom! My stomach clenched. How was I going to explain leaving school to her and Dad?

It might work better if the news came from Westenburg. I pulled out my notebook.

Dear Mr. and Mrs. Antonucci: I have given Kaitlyn this letter to give to you.

Two "gives" in one sentence wasn't great, but then, Westenburg wasn't known for his writing.

I am sorry to report to you that Martin Van Buren Middle School does not seem to be the appropriate place for her. While Kaitlyn used to be an exemplary student, last year she frequently appeared stupefied. I ~~hesitate to recommend~~ strongly disrecommend parochial school for a girl with her ORIGINAL AND CURIOUS MIND?? STRONG INDEPENDENT—

No. I was done with faking and pretending and lying. I grabbed up a stick and dug through the leaves until I reached dirt, then scraped at it till I'd made a hole. When the stick broke, I used a flat rock to make the hole bigger. But that felt too slow, so I dug with my hands. When it looked like it was big enough to hold everything, I put in the notebook, squashing my lunch bag down on top of it. Then I threw in Tyler's hat, put back the soil and the leaves, wiped my hands on my jeans, and started running again—off the path now, and into the thicket that came out at the stone wall at the beginning of my road.

I'd spent half an hour at Staples, though, picking out that notebook. It was the perfect notebook. So I ran back again. I worried I wouldn't find the hole, but the log was easy to spot, and so were the disturbed leaves. In less than a minute, I'd dug up the notebook, torn out the letter, ripped it to pieces, and stuffed it in Tyler's hat along with the tuna sandwich. Then I refilled the hole and stamped it down. Then I dusted off the notebook and wrote on the first page:

This is the DISCOVERY JOURNAL of
KATYA ANTONUCCI

I wished there wasn't that stupid "ucci" on the end. "Katya Anton" could be a poet, or a writer, or a special agent. "Katya Antonucci" looked ludicrous.

Well—I took a deep breath—too bad.

Sept 5, 9:02 a.m. I wrote. Katya Antonucci lives. Then I burst into tears.

9

3

I almost cried again when I got home. I didn't dare risk going inside, though, so I cut around back to my brothers' old tree house. It put me a little too close for comfort to Mom's salon—the salon was upstairs over the garage—but I was well hidden by the leaves, and the sunshine filtering through the branches of the old oak made it amazingly peaceful. Plus, I discovered, after I'd braved a dash to the house for the laptop, the Internet worked. I could tell Rosie! Because Rosie wouldn't be at school either. She hadn't been to school a day in her life. She homeschooled. Which I hadn't paid that much attention to at camp, but now . . .

 NatureGirl: rosie r u sitting down?

I LEFT SCHOOL!!!!!!

ur the first to know. now i have to tell my parents. HELP!!!! do NOT call my home #, which rings in my moms salon as well as in the house. she doesnt know im not at school today. dont even call my cell. shes got the windows open.

xoxoxoxoxxoxoxoxoxoxoxoxoxoxoxoxoxo

ps if u have any ideas at all, send ASAP!!!!!

pps pls send me everything u know about homeschooling

ppps how r u?

✉ To: Dimitri_Olshansky@umass.edu

Subject: !!

guess what, dimitri? i'm homeschooling!

Now, who else could I tell who'd be excited for me?

I couldn't think of anyone.

Somewhere near my ear, a mosquito whined. In the branches above me some bird went, *Birdy, birdy, birdy.* Footsteps clumped down the stairs; Mom's nine o'clock must be leaving. Oh, no! And now Waffle was barking. I didn't know he was outside! I sniffed under my arm, praying I didn't smell from my run; beagles have great noses.

"Some watchdog, right?" I heard Mom say. "Only barks when someone's leaving."

A car door slammed. More footsteps. Her ten o'clock arriving.

Eight hours to come up with a plan. Where was Rosie?

I had only one idea so far. Dad and Mom were huge do-it-yourselfers. Not just this tree house, with its neat built-in benches with storage underneath, fold-down table, and a pulley for hoisting up supplies. They'd done all the construction on the beauty shop, poured the cement for the patio, made the raised beds in the vegetable garden. They watched the DIY Channel every night, not to mention the

Food Network. Give them the instructions or the recipe and they'd tackle anything. But I couldn't waltz in and say, "Hey, if you guys can make a turducken for Thanksgiving, we can handle do-it-yourself school."

Plus, neither one was what you'd call alternative, or open to new ideas, unless it was their idea. They didn't take it well that I applied to Wilderness Discovery without telling them, even when I won the essay contest and got the scholarship. And that was camp, not homeschool.

IMPORTANT!!!

I wrote in my notebook.

DO NOT make eye contact with M first.
Start w/ D instead.
DO NOT cry, shout, or lose my temper.
DO NOT do anything where they can say
"there she goes again being so extreme/
melodramatic/a drama queen/a teenager."
NO stupid stories or lame excuses.
DO NOT go in unprepared. "WHEN IN DOUBT,
WRITE IT OUT."

That sounded so right, it made my heart race. Maybe not just write out notes for myself. Write up all my reasons for leaving. Document them. In a document.

⌨ Remember how you didn't want me to go to camp? Well, if I hadn't seen that wildlife magazine in Dr. Roberts's waiting room, and read about the essay contest, we'd have never known Wilderness Discovery existed! And it's not like I was ever this big nature/science person, but something in me <u>knew</u> it was the <u>exact right place</u> for me. And you guys may have had your doubts, but you <u>trusted</u> me. And it turned out to be way better than I even dreamed! So when I tell you that I have the same feeling about homeschooling, you should trust me now too.

No. Bad. I should start lighter, ease them into it.

WORST REASON TO STAY IN SCHOOL
"School prepares you for life. If you can't drag your butt into a boring class every day, how do you expect to drag your butt into a job you hate?"
—Uncle Anthony

Better. I kept going:

REASONS FOR LEAVING
1. So I can look forward to getting up in the morning
2. So I can stand to get up in the morning
3. So that you will never, I swear, have to say the word "surly" again!

**THINGS YOU WILL NOT HAVE TO WORRY
ABOUT ANYMORE**

1. My happiness (see above)
2. Bad influences (except for you! ☺)
3. Tyler Anderson

I deleted that one. Tyler was already history. But I wondered if I dared put in something about my "bad attitude" at school, my "acting out behavior." Explain how it was kind of hard to stop when so many kids liked me so much better that way. Admit that I was worried I'd get so good at acting dumb and stupid, it would no longer be an act. But then they'd demand details. I'd have to get specific. And even without knowing about the letters Mr. Westenburg sent home, they'd be so mad, they wouldn't read another word. And I'd end up at Immaculate Heart of Mary, with the nuns.

🖥 WHY SCHOOL IS UNNECESSARY

Rosie Hoffman-Grainger hasn't gone to school in her entire life. She knows more about more things than anyone my age I have ever met. I have never seen her without a book. She is also happy, has high self-esteem, is never bored or cynical, does not have a foul mouth, tattoos, or weird hair, or have a sketchy boyfriend, gets along excellently with her parents, and has no authority issues. Rosie Hoffman-Grainger will be my role model.

Uh-oh! Voices! My stomach dropped as I peered over

the tree house wall. A blue-haired lady was coming out of the salon. A lady who looked scarily like Ms. Pinchbeck. What was she doing here during school hours? I stopped breathing, listening for my name as Mom stepped onto the landing with her. I was practically at eye level with them.

"I never thought I'd like it this short," I heard Ms. Pinchbeck say.

"I told you, Aida!" Mom said.

Eew. I couldn't believe anyone would hug Aida Pinchbeck. Even if my theory about her hair being a wig was not true.

I moved into the far corner of the tree house and crouched there biting the skin around my thumbnails while they chatted. I didn't hear my name, thank God, but I heard the word *tomatoes.*

Do not go down the stairs, Mom! Do not show her the garden! Then Waffle would follow them, and find me, and . . .

At last I heard Ms. Pinchbeck say, "Well, duty calls," and then a car door slam.

My cuticles were bleeding. How could it be almost noon already? Even with a huge font and wide margins, I had less than two pages.

NatureGirl: rosie, i thought homeschooling meant u were at home! ru there, rosie?

AN EXAMPLE OF SOMETHING EXTREMELY INTERESTING TO ME THAT I HEARD ABOUT AT CAMP AND PLAN TO DO A PROJECT ON

MOM AND DAD PLEASE NOTE: I wrote this just now

15

so that you can see what I'll be able to do <u>all the time</u>, now that I won't be buried in <u>repetitive, mindless make-work</u>.

TEENAGE BRAINS

In case you are wondering, it isn't just hormones making me emotional, irrational, and hard to manage. Even as we speak, my teenage brain is getting physically restructured to prepare me for being an adult. While some parts are growing rapidly, others are being pruned, in the course of which some of the higher reasoning processes somehow get messed up, and the part of the brain responsible for emotions takes over.

In other words, the mess in teens' rooms, lockers, and backpacks only reflects what's in their heads. Furthermore, teens who veg out in school are losing parts of the brain that could be used for acquiring knowledge and understanding.

But this DOES NOT have to happen. Teens whose brains are STIMULATED will MAKE new neural connections, not LOSE them. THEY WILL GET SMARTER, NOT DUMBER . . .

And now it was quarter to two. The mosquitoes were eating me alive. I desperately needed the bathroom. And I was so hungry! At least Mom hadn't gone back to the house for lunch and found her laptop gone.

But now here was Waffle with his paws up on the ladder,

whining. Any second, he'd be tangled in his rope and doing his whole beagle baying thing.

"Quiet, Waffle," I begged as I climbed down the ladder. "Good boy." I stroked his ears and gave his head a scratch. "Come on, Waf. Be cool. I'm getting us something to eat." With him trotting eagerly alongside, I ran to Dad's vegetable garden and picked a bunch of cucumbers and tomatoes, threw him two cukes and, ignoring his piteous howls, climbed back up again with my vegetables. He was still right under me, but at least he was lying down. Trying not to squirt tomato guts on the laptop, I reread what I had so far. More than I thought. But it was all about me. Nothing about homeschool. I needed facts, figures, success stories.

Fortunately, the Web was loaded with them. In half an hour, I'd downloaded a whole bunch of impressive-looking articles and FAQs to add to my presentation. Then, because I was starting to feel way better, I wrote on a stand-alone new page:

💻 Just so you know: I've already done more on my own today than I did all last year at school.

I was beginning a list of things I'd gotten interested in at camp, or thought I might get interested in—edible wild plants, coyotes, the human brain, karate, poetry, art, music, literature, Eastern philosophy—when Rosie's message popped up.

Rosebud: OMG! ur gonna homeschool????? im excited!! only ques: how well do u get along with yr mom + dad??? if they r gonna wanna b yr teachers, u will b spending A LOT of time w/ them.

Rosebud: sorry i took so long to answer. just got home from african dance class and zen archery. (no, k, homeschool doesn't mean u always stay at home!)

Teachers? What a jerk I was not to have thought of that! If any do-it-yourselfing was going on, they'd want to be the do-ers. But neither of them had ever taught, or even gone to college, or knew anything about the human brain or Eastern philosophy or karate. Or the first thing about coyotes. Not to mention that they both worked all day.

No! I couldn't think about that now!

NatureGirl: i'll make it work, r, don't worry

"Kaitlyn?" Mom's worried face appeared at the top of the ladder. "What are you doing up there? Why aren't you in school?"

CHAPTER

4

"Early dismissal."

The words slipped from my lips so easily, it sounded true even to me.

Mom my teacher? That might work for Rosie. One of her moms was a writer, the other a psychologist. When I saw them at camp, they looked very intelligent. Although people in skinny little glasses and Birkenstocks do tend to look brainier than people in pressed elastic-waist jeans, frosted hair, and ankle bracelets. Not that I knew Mom was wearing her ankle bracelet. At the moment I could only see her from the shoulders up.

"Subjects to study," she read off the laptop screen before I could minimize. "You're doing homework already?"

"Uh . . ." I seemed to have used up all my tricky answers. She was looking kind of hopeful and friendly, though, so I took a chance. "It's actually something to show you and Dad." She'd like that. I never showed them anything, ever.

"About neuroscience?"

She looked surprised and pleased. Maybe I was too quick with those snobby thoughts. She'd done really well in high school. She read constantly. She beat everyone, including me, at Boggle.

"It's sort of a surprise," I said. "For later."

"The day I've had," she said, "I could use a nice surprise." She climbed the last few rungs of the ladder and stepped onto the platform.

This wasn't part of my plan, but I moved my legs over to make room for her.

"What is it about the first day of school?" she said, sitting on the bench across from me. "You can be forty years old or eighty, when school starts up, you want a makeover." She pulled a pack of cigarettes from her pocket and tapped one out. "It's only my third one," she said, though I hadn't said anything. She lit up and took a long, grateful drag. "Every single person who came in today was like, 'Make me look different.' And I'm like, 'Ok-aay, so what'd you have in mind?' And they're like, 'I don't know. Just make me look better. I want to look youthful.' I mean, excuse me? Aida Pinchbeck?"

My stomach turned over. "She didn't say anything about me, did she?"

Mom snorted. "Are you kidding? She was too busy thinking about the new youthful her."

Whew.

"So instead of cutting off a quarter inch, I take off half, and put on a tiny dab of product, and she still looks exactly the same as when I was in junior high, but she's like, 'Oh, Donna, I don't know why anyone would pay two hundred dollars to get their hair done in New York when they can come right here to you, for thirty.'" She waved the smoke away from me. "Then there's Shirley Jacobs, with the pictures of her dogs, and Millie Loomis, with barely enough hair left to cut, and Ed Horton's pedicure. The man should go to a podiatrist, not a beauty parlor! And I still have three more cuts coming in today and, guess what? Tomorrow I get to do it all again! I should have been a dentist. At least their clients can't talk to them."

"You could always, like, stuff cotton in their mouths," I said. "Or give them laughing gas."

"Give myself laughing gas. So how was your first day? Less annoying than mine, I hope."

"Well . . ." I took a deep breath. "You don't have to worry about me and Tyler anymore. It's over. For real this time."

"Oh, yeah?" I could see her trying to decide if she dared say what she thought, or, since we were getting along better than we had since camp, leave it alone. She looked me over. "You seem kind of weird. Other than Tyler, was school okay?"

My stomach flipped again. "Yeah. You know, Mom, maybe you need to raise your rates."

"Or take a vacation. Or find another line of work. And how likely is that?"

I sat up. "Are you serious?" It had never dawned on me that Mom might be as trapped as I was.

I'd thought I was done writing, but as soon as she climbed down for her next client, I started a new document:

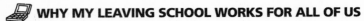 **WHY MY LEAVING SCHOOL WORKS FOR ALL OF US**

1. I'm not the only one who's ready for a new challenge. Mom said herself her work is boring and annoying, and she is not getting paid enough.
2. If we are both less stupefied and frustrated we won't get on each other's nerves and (Dad, take note!!) Mom will stop smoking.

I debated putting that in, but it was ridiculous for her to pretend Dad didn't know.

3. We get along really well and enjoy each other's company. We could have a nice time together, the way we used to. Without laughing gas.

I actually used to love those afternoons with her. I'd run straight from the bus to the salon, grab a handful of Jolly Ranchers from the bowl by the coffeemaker, and then listen to her chat with clients while I read *Celebrity Hairstyles* or, since I was good back then, did homework. Between clients, she'd give me a manicure, or play around with my hair. When I wanted my ears pierced, she did it for me. When I wanted two more holes in the left ear, she made those too, and pierced her own to match. She always seemed to know what I wanted to look like—not froufy, or girly, but not a tomboy either, and always different from my friends. But then, I was into all that back in those days.

📟 Mom: I'm not saying you can do my hair again ☺.
But I feel like maybe we could have fun like that the way
we used to.

When I got back to the house, I removed the pages from
two of Dad's loose-leaf home repair manuals, printed two
copies of all my pages—with all the articles I'd found, I had
a lot of pages!—punched holes and arranged them in the
binders. Then I made up the title page:

📟 THE ULTIMATE DO-IT-YOURSELF PROJECT
by KAITYLN ANTONUCCI

Whoa! I thought as I taped it to the binder. Why had
I thought Mom had to teach me? Dad loved explaining
things, even if most of the things he wanted to explain
weren't things I wanted to know, like what was inside my
computer, or how to make beer or turn yard waste into
compost. So what if he was at work? Rosie's moms worked
too. We'd do this the way they did. I made a note to find
out what that was, and tell her about being my role model.
Then I went back to the computer, added a whole paragraph about Dad, and ended:

📟 I am a self-starter. (I could start to be a self-starter ☺.)

Then I was so pumped, I went back and changed the
"Kaitlyn" on the title page to "Katya."

Hmmm … Should I tell my friends I'd changed my name? Or my brothers? I owed Sean and Tommy e-mails anyway. Maybe not yet. One bombshell at a time. I shot off a quick message to everyone I could think of, including Tyler:

✉ guess what??? i wanted u to hear it from me first. do not look 4 me at school 2moro or anymore. im homeschooling. i will miss u all, but NOT the place. details l8r. LYL, K.

Would they be even slightly happy for me? I was suddenly too excited to care. I deleted the "miss" and "love you lots" part from Tyler's. I added a line to my brothers asking them if they were still liking their jobs, and if Sean Jr.'s tooth had come in, and telling them to cross their fingers for when I told Mom and Dad. Then I washed up, fixed my hair, and put on the skirt Mom had bought me for the first day, which I'd refused to wear this morning. I made up a plate of cheese and crackers. I stuck a new bottle of Chardonnay in the fridge for Mom, and some bottles of beer for Dad from the batch he'd made the Fourth of July when my brothers drove down from Maine. I fed Waffle extra chow so he'd go to sleep, so that in case this didn't go the way I hoped, he wouldn't start to bark and chase his tail the way he did when things got loud. I even swept the kitchen floor.

I had a brief panic about using Dad's repair manuals for my binders. But it was too late to do anything about it. Dad was home.

CHAPTER 5

"Cheese and crackers anyone? Is your drink okay? Dad, got your reading glasses?" I'd brought everything out to the screened porch so that Dad couldn't turn on the six o'clock news, and Mom wouldn't get distracted fixing dinner. "Have a seat. Relax. Take a load off."

Take a load off? Was this me talking? My heart hammered as I waited for them to settle themselves at the table.

"Ta-da!" I handed each of them a binder.

"Wait a minute." Dad's hand paused halfway to the beer bottle. "Is this my washing machine repair manual? And my dishwasher instructions? What'd you do with the pages, Kaity? You didn't throw them out, did you?"

"No, no. They're in my room, Dad. I just borrowed the binders." I should have told him that first off. I forced a smile and tried to decide if I'd do better standing up or sitting down. "Just read what I wrote, okay? Starting with the title."

Nerves twanging, I sat down across from them.

"Katya, eh?" His amused look made me think of the tea parties I used to have when I was little, where I'd sit Mom and Dad on the edge of the sandbox, give them dish towels for their laps, then offer Kool-Aid from my Fisher-Price tea set and pass around sand crumpets decorated with barberries.

"What is this?" Mom said. "What does this mean, 'reasons for leaving'? Kaity, if this is your surprise, I'm gonna need more than a glass of Chardonnay."

"Okay." Dad leaned back in his chair and folded his arms. My dad's a big guy. When his eyes lose that amused gleam and zoom in on you, he seems even bigger. "What happened?"

"Nothing *happened*." I'd been so sure I'd at least get an "Oh, wow!" about how many pages I'd written, and how great the binders looked. I leaned across the table and flipped to my introduction. "Just read it. It's all explained, right here."

His eyebrows were knit together in that way I hate. "You don't just decide you're not going to school. We'll call you any name you want. Just tell us what's going on."

"I mean, you told me you broke up with Tyler . . ." Mom said.

No one had touched the cheese. The last time Dad left food sitting on a plate was when Uncle Anthony got divorced.

"This has nothing to do with Tyler," I said. "It's about me. And you guys. And education—"

"Did you have a fight with someone?" Dad asked. "Are you getting picked on?"

"I remember when I was in junior high," Mom said, "and I was already pretty developed, like you, and these jerks would drive around after me calling crude things out the window—"

"You sure that wasn't me, hon?" Dad said, clearly trying to lighten things up. But only for a second. "I mean it, Kaity. Is somebody giving you a hard time? Are your friends into stuff you don't want to tell us? I don't like to say this, but did somebody do something, you know, inappropriate?"

"No!" I'd been trying so hard to stay calm. "I told you! Nothing happened. There's no illegal substances. Mr. Westenburg didn't expose himself in the file room. No one is bullying me." I cut a slice of brie and stuck it on a cracker. But it felt like I was going to choke on it, my throat was so tight. I stood up. "School's just not working for me. Can't you understand that? I can't be there. That's what this whole binder is saying, if you'd just—"

"Not working for you?" Mom said. "You're getting good grades, you're in the marching band, the phone rings off the hook—"

"With people I don't particularly want—"

"And since when was it about school working for you?" Dad said. "Going to school *is* your work. If I was half as good at it as you, you think I'd still be selling lawn tractors?"

"I thought you loved your friends," Mom said.

"I do, but I'm not like them anymore."

"Then maybe you need to make some new friends," she

27

said. "What about Francesca Halloran? She was always a very smart girl. You never mention her any—"

"And I'm not gonna lie," Dad said. "I always thought Tyler was kind of a dim bulb."

"Would you stop talking about Tyler?" I was gripping the iron chair back so hard, my hands ached. "It's not about Tyler, or my friends, or playing the stupid piccolo in the stupid marching band! I'm learning nothing there. I can't take another year of watching the minute hand, counting the hairs on my arms, getting in stupid trouble!"

Uh-oh.

"Whoa!" Dad half rose in his seat. "What do you mean, getting in trouble?"

Mom's eyes had gone all dark. "What trouble, Kaitlyn?"

"Nothing like what you're thinking!" My brothers spent the night in jail one Halloween for turning over gravestones. My cousin Nicole "got in trouble" her senior year, married the guy from the convenience store, and is now divorced with three kids. "You're always jumping to these ridiculous, extreme conclusions! I'm not going back to school!" I shouted. "I can't do it!"

Dad almost never raises his voice; he just says the same thing over and over. But you shout at Mom, she shouts back at you. So there's Waffle charging down the breezeway from the kitchen, dashing from one of us to the other, yipping and baying, and Mom yelling, "Me, extreme? You're the one refusing to go to school!" and "I knew this would happen, Joe! I knew if we let her go to that camp . . ." and me waving

28

my arms, hollering, "I'm trying to tell you something AND YOU'RE NOT LISTENING!"

All we needed now was for Grandpa to walk through the door and say homeschooling was for hippies and Communists.

"If you give him a biscuit you're just rewarding him for bad behavior!" Mom yelled as I grabbed Waffle by the collar and pulled him toward the kitchen.

I gave him a biscuit. I drank some water. I counted to ten, and ten again. Then I tried to decide whether to go back and tell them how much I hated them, or go up to my room and get under the covers and never come out.

Mom had opened the sliders and was outside smoking a cigarette when I got back, with her shoulders in their angry up position. But Dad was still at the table. He seemed to be reading what I'd written. I closed my eyes and took a long, slow, supposedly cleansing breath the way I'd learned at camp. The blood was still pounding in my ears, but I walked over to the sofa, plunked myself down, picked up one of the puffy green-pink-and-white-flowered cushions, and wrapped my arms around it.

"You want to know what happened?" I said. "I got to school this morning and my body just couldn't be there. It was like, No. This can't be what I'm supposed to be doing with my life. There has to be something better." My voice trembled. "Haven't you ever felt like that, Dad? Haven't you ever felt like something in your life is just too wrong to bear?"

He didn't answer, but when Mom turned around, her eyes had changed.

"And I mean, before camp, I knew I wasn't happy. But I didn't know there was anything else." Mom ground out her cigarette and came back inside and sat down on the sofa next to me. I didn't look at her. "For seven years I've been under so much pressure, Mom, to act a certain way and look a certain way, and get good grades, but not so good that people will hate me and I'll never have a boyfriend. And like, totally stand out, but never by questioning anything or arguing with a teacher. At camp, smart was a good thing. They wanted you to question everything. Here smart either equals geek, or know-it-all, or suck-up, or smart-ass troublemaker."

I sat there and waited for someone to say something.

"Kaity, honey," Dad said finally. "We can't afford private school. And we don't have an alternative school here. We have Martin Van Buren, and Immaculate Heart, where I frankly don't see you being happy."

"I'm not asking to go to private school," I said.

"You think your mom can close the salon to teach you all day? You think I can quit work to be your teacher? Even if I could, I wouldn't, because A, I'm not smart enough—"

"You are too!" I said. "You're very smart."

"Not at school things. B, I'm not a teacher. C, I don't remember half of what I learned in school."

"Half?" Mom snorted. "You're doing better than I am."

"Plus, even if we could find a way to do it," he said, "you'd be miserable. Forget band. There'd be no more sports or dances. You'd be home alone all day instead of with people your age. Or worse, with Mom." He looked at her. "No offense, honey."

Mom touched my shoulder. "But you put so much effort into this booklet, sweetie. Maybe you can use some of it for something else. A school project or something . . ."

I just looked at her. "You haven't even read it."

I went out to the tree house and sat there in the dark with the mosquitoes.

After a while, Dad came and asked if I wanted dinner.

"Come on, Kaitykins," he called up to me. "I know you're disappointed, but you've gotta be realistic. We'll go in to school with you tomorrow morning and have a talk with Westenburg."

"Westenburg?" I shouted. "Why don't we just have a talk with Waffle?"

When I finally came back in, I could hear the TV going. "Who will be the winner of tonight's Battle Spinach? Whose cuisine reigns supreme?" They'd left pasta and some salad for me on the counter, but I had no appetite.

After a while the TV went off. I heard the light click on in their bedroom, and them talking in low voices. I tiptoed to their door. Dad was still trying to convince Mom or himself that everybody hated middle school, he'd certainly hated middle school, but you live through it and then you get to high school and you have a blast. "Plus, remember how it was when you were Kaity's age? You have a bad day, and it's the end of the world. Then some cute boy says hi to you . . ."

Vermont! Rosie's! The bus schedule online said there was a bus at eight tomorrow from New Haven, sixty-one dollars for an adult, round trip. Counting the thirteen birthday silver dollars from Grandpa, I had enough money. A cab to New Haven would be expensive, but with my hair in two braids, and a baggy top, maybe I could pass for under twelve and go half fare on the bus.

"Would you please just relax and go to sleep, Donna." Dad's voice was loud enough for me to hear him through the wall. "Remember how she cried her eyes out over leaving Tyler Anderson to go to camp? And then it was camp she was crying about leaving? What I'm saying is, if we don't jump in with all four feet and turn this into a whole big thing, she could forget about it by morning."

"You're right," Mom said. "I mean, I changed my name too when I was her age. It pissed me off no end when Pop wouldn't call me Jennifer."

That's when I decided I didn't want a round trip. I pulled my blanket off the bed, eased open my door, and tiptoed down the stairs. Waffle padded after me expectantly. "Shhh! I'm just going to the tree house," I told him. But as soon as I was out the door, my feet headed for the road.

It was all woods and farms here when Mom and Dad were growing up. Now it was mostly houses, but except for a few lighted windows, and the moon, half covered with clouds, the road was totally dark and quiet. Also, somewhat scary. But I wrapped the blanket around myself and kept walking, to the end of our development, where the woods started and the trees overhung the road. Tree frogs chirped. The katydids were making their end-of-summer *bee-bee-beep-boo-boo-boop!* racket. A deerfly whined around my ears. I pulled the blanket higher and walked faster, till the woods opened out into fields. I could hear rustlings in the grass. Snakes slept at night, I told myself. It was just chipmunks, or mice; even tiny animals made loud, scary rustles. I wished now I'd brought Waffle, and a flashlight. But I kept going, walking uphill now, to the big, rocky, overgrown pasture everyone called Alvin's field. The clouds had moved away from the moon. A few stars glimmered.

I was standing there in the road thinking, *Well, if I can walk a mile alone in the pitch dark, the bus to Rosie's will be nothing,* when a yowling scream pierced the air. I froze. It felt like it was coming from the field. The hairs on the back of my neck prickled as whatever it was screeched again. It didn't sound like any coyote I'd ever heard. I'd just decided screech owl when it morphed into music, violin music, really gorgeous music, like something you'd hear at a concert. Then it changed again, to rasps and screaks, like the violin was cursing or vomiting.

I gathered the blanket tighter around me, imagining a lonely, crazed, white-bearded hermit in a raggedy tuxedo standing on the big rock at the top of the hill, sparks shooting from his eyes as he played.

A wild, roaring cry rang out—a cry so pained I could feel it in my throat. Before I could stop myself my mouth opened. "Yaaaaaaaahhhhhh!" I scream-roared along with him even as I ran down the hill toward home. "Yaaaaaaaahhhhhh!"

CHAPTER

NatureGirl: shoot me now, rosie! i missed the bus!!!! dunno if the alarm didn't go off or what but 5 a.m. came and went so im still here and now theyre waiting to take me to see the principal.

#$%%^&&**&* @#$%%^&&**&! Dad's pounding on the door. Gtg.

IF U NEVER HEAR FROM ME AGAIN, U WILL KNOW THAT I AM DEAD!

The office smelled like old perfume, and the Lysol Ms. Pinchbeck used to spray the phones, and fear. Which was probably me.

But it wasn't just being here at school that scared me now. The only times I'd seen Dad look like this was when he got pulled over for speeding. I'd never seen Mom bite her nails. Even before she said hello to Pinchbeck, she was assuring her my shoes were in the car. Because I had on flip-flops—horrors! A dress code violation! I'd also refused to bring my backpack. Which they'd put in the car too, along with the shoes. Which was why we were twenty-five minutes later than they wanted. Which was fine with me, since it meant first period had already started, and I didn't have to face anyone. I still hadn't answered the fourteen alarmed messages from my friends last night. Or the one from Tyler:

📱 hey. i know ur not ditching school cuza me ☺. cuz i still have feelings for you.

Ms. Pinchbeck frowned again at the flip-flops as we followed Mr. Westenburg into the inner office.

"Donna, you're looking lovely, as always," he said in his hearty I'm-your-friend voice as he pulled three chairs into a semicircle around his desk. I took the one closest to the door. "Same Donna as when you were in my World Geography class. Joseph, I like that fall display you've got out in front of the store. Was that your doing?" Dad nodded as if he'd been given a gold star. "It's very nice," said Mr. Westenburg. "Very . . . fall-like." He shut the door and perched on the corner of his desk and crossed his legs. "And how are you, Kaitlyn?"

Westenburg looks like an extremely large, rotund baby, with a smooth, pink face, a few fine, wispy gray hairs that he glues across his scalp, and a forehead that looks like he shined it with a shoeshine rag. Or, as I said in another of my infamous letters, Ms. Pinchbeck polishes it for him. I also drew a picture of him as an evil Humpty Dumpty in a giant Pamper. That one, luckily, he never saw.

My voice came out way too wimpy. "Not that good," I said.

"Then I'm glad you came to me," he said.

I threw Mom and Dad a Can-we-leave-yet? look. They were so focused on him, they didn't notice.

"I was hoping to see you here last year," he told them. "So we could deal with some of Kaitlyn's issues. But since this is a fresh new year, let's get off to a fresh start. How's that sound, Kaitlyn? You know Kaitlyn is a very special girl. Bright, and vivacious, and full of spunk, just like her mom."

"Thank you," Mom said. She'd put on good slacks for the meeting, and a twinset, even though it was way too warm for any sweater at all. "But could we back up a second? What issues?"

"Yeah," Dad said. "Is there some problem we don't know about?"

Westenburg looked puzzled. "You didn't get the letters I sent home?"

I hadn't had a stomachache since last year. My head was starting to hurt too.

"As I like to tell students"—Westenburg eased himself off the desk and lumbered to the row of file cabinets along the side wall—"we're a learning community here, a learning partnership, where every voice is valued. Our mission"—he pulled open a drawer—"is to provide a challenging, enriching experience and foster a lifetime passion for learning."

I could feel myself wanting to numb over and blank out. I didn't dare, not with Mom and Dad nodding so solemnly, even though his back was to them.

"However . . . challenges of adolescence . . . negative behavior . . ."—his voice picked up steam as he got to the bad stuff—"failure to apply herself . . . disruptive influence . . . difficulty staying on task . . . necessary interventions . . ."

I prayed my file was lost. No. He'd found it.

"I won't read you chapter and verse," he said, opening the folder. "Just give you a sense of the problem. Reading books under the desk . . . passing notes . . . drawing rude pictures . . . slept through test review . . ."

"Don't all kids do that?" Dad said. "I mean, I sure did."

It was the first sign of life from either of them in a while.

Westenburg narrowed his eyes at Dad as if to say, *And look at you today,* and kept reading: ". . . skipped early-morning review sessions. . . contradicted her teacher . . . questions assignments . . . refuses to read the books on the AR list . . . ignores guidelines regarding headings and margins—"

I couldn't believe Mom raised her hand. "Excuse me. Headings and margins? I mean, she does great on all the tests. Her report cards are mostly A's. Do these things you're calling problems really matter?"

"Not per se, Donna," he said, "but I'm afraid it's part of a larger pattern. And I know you're thinking, Yes, but she's more gifted than the other students, but unfortunately, we can't custom-tailor a curriculum or bend the rules. I wish we could, Donna, but we just can't. Not with twenty-nine students in a class, and federal and state mandates. But that's why we developed the Resource Center, with two enrichment specialists, where students are invited to work independently on projects of their choice. But, and correct me if I'm wrong, Kaitlyn, she chose not to take advantage of that."

"Yes, but—" I started.

"There were also more serious incidents," he said. "Which the letters cite. Notably, Valentine's Day, when she circulated a highly inappropriate, you could even say offensive, letter."

"About what?" Mom said.

His face reddened. "Nothing we need go into here. There was also the textbook incident, where she hid a certain teacher's teacher's edition and the entire period was wasted searching for it."

"Yes, but—" I tried again.

This time it was Dad who cut me off. "Mr. Westenburg, would you excuse us for a minute? Kaitlyn, we need to talk to you outside."

Next thing I knew he had me by the arm and was hustling me to the parking lot.

"I never, ever contradicted a teacher unless I knew they were wrong!" I told him. "I can work perfectly well independently," I told Mom, who was hurrying to keep up with us. "If it's not a stupid task, I stay on task just fine. Ground me for a year. Throw my phone away. I'll clean the toilets for the rest of my life. Just, please, don't—"

We were at the car now. Dad leaned against it and folded his arms across his chest. His eyebrows bunched together in an angry line. His eyes zoomed in on me. "Here I was worried bad things were happening to you," he said. "Come to find out you're the one doing the bad things. Better tell us what was in the offensive letter, Kaity, and what happened to those letters he sent us."

Several lie possibilities jumped to mind. But part of me was relieved the truth was finally coming out.

"I stuck them in the stump," I said. "Behind the mailbox. There's this like really deep hole in it. Tommy and Sean used to hide stuff there too, and I, like, shoved them all the way in, but if you want . . ." They both stood there, waiting, I knew, for me to stop blathering and tell them about the quote, offensive letter, unquote. "It was just this stupid thing I wrote, about how Westenburg had twelve toes and was having a secret love affair. But I didn't circulate it. It just sort of got around—"

"Got around?" Mom's voice rose. "No wonder he has a file on you!"

"Yes, but it wasn't me who read it over the PA system. It was this little jerk Jessie was dating, Danny Wasserman. And I told Westenburg I was sorry, and I apologized to Ms. Pinchbeck."

Mom's eyes bugged out. "Ms. Pinchbeck?"

I made a sheepish face. "I may have implied that they were lovers."

"This is bad," Dad said. "Really bad. It doesn't even sound like you."

"That's what I've been trying to tell you!" My voice was shrill in my ears. "It's what school's doing to me! I saw it doing it to you too, in there. It's like you guys totally forgot who you were. I mean, you were sitting there like he was God, and we were worms—"

His look shut me up.

"Is there anything else we need to know?" he said. "Before we go back in and face this guy again?"

"Yeah. That thing he said about hiding Ms. Novak's teacher's edition? It was a joke. But I was trying to make a point, which is that she can't teach without it. And maybe I don't read AR books, but you see me reading all the time, right? And that Resource Room? They stuck the two worst teachers in the school there. To get them out of a real classroom. Kids just go in there and use their phone, or play video games, or sleep. I went in there once and Ms. Young—"

"The Ms. Young Sean and Tommy had for English?" Mom stopped digging in her purse for her cigarettes. "The one the kids always used to make cry?"

"Exactly. And remember Mr. Morabito? With the nervous tics?" I demonstrated. "And the anger management issues?"

"Come on, you know you had some good teachers," Dad said. "Maybe you just got a few bad eggs last year."

"Yeah, some of them were fine," I said. "That's not the point. The point is I learned nothing! And I don't know if they couldn't tell, or they didn't care as long as I went through the motions. If I hadn't stopped going along, Westenburg would never have known either. And I might be everything he says, but that's not what I want to be, Dad. I'm trying to be something good here . . ."

My words hung there, pompous, desperate.

Mom and Dad looked at each other. Dad took out his

cell phone and punched in a number. "Everything under control there, Al?" he said into it. "Good. 'Cause this is taking a little longer than I thought." He hung up. "Kaity, why don't you wait for us over by the door."

I did, but it was close enough that I could still hear them talking.

"So what are we gonna do?" he asked Mom.

I was afraid to breathe.

"You think I know?" she said. "I have to tell you, though, it really irks me that he never even asked why we were here. And all that hot air about 'learning partnerships' and 'passion for learning'? Did you ever hear such a load of bull in your life? And did you believe that headings and margins crap?"

"This isn't about him, Donna," Dad said. "But I have to say, I didn't care for the way he implied that Kaity doesn't apply herself."

"Imply it? Joe, he said it! And did you see the way she was clutching her stomach?"

"You stuck the binder in her backpack, right?" he said. "You think she'd let us show him what she wrote? He needs to hear our side."

Our side? Tears sprang to my eyes.

So, even though I hadn't planned on anyone but them seeing it, I called, "Yeah. Go ahead. Show it to him."

"I'm not saying there's any excuse for what Kaity did," Dad told Westenburg when we got back. We didn't sit this time. "And if you'd like a written apology from her, we'll see you get one. But you say Kaitlyn doesn't apply herself? Well, I have to disagree with you. See this?" He held out the binder. "She wrote this whole thing yesterday."

Westenburg flipped through the pages. Except for a tightening of his lips, his face didn't change.

"Pretty impressive, isn't it?" Dad said. "And pretty disturbing."

"You got that right!" Mom nodded. "A girl who's so turned off by school she'd leave her friends and give up all her activities to try something we know nothing about?"

"I agree, Joseph," Westenburg said. "She did an impressive amount of work. Which goes to show what she can do when she's motivated. But surely you're not considering homeschooling. I have the highest opinion of you both, you know that, and you were both fine students, but let's be frank, you're not exactly—"

"Exactly what?" Mom's eyes contracted to two dark little points. "Are you saying we're not up to the job? Are you saying we're not smart enough—"

Westenburg put up a hand. "Not at all. But you're not teachers, and correct me if I'm wrong, but neither of you even went to—"

"We may not be teachers, Harold," Mom said. "But I feel like we could do a better job than you people. I mean, please. Headings and margins?"

"I honestly don't know what we're considering at this point," Dad said. "But this place clearly isn't working for her."

It was all I could do not to hurl myself into their arms.

"I guess I'd send her to private school if we had the money," Dad said.

Westenburg waved that away. "You'd never get her in at this time of year. I assume you're going to leave her here till you decide?"

Mom made a sound like the air coming out of a balloon. "I don't think so."

"Well, in that case," he said, "you'll need to send in a letter withdrawing her from the public schools. At that point, under Connecticut law, you have ten days to file your Notice of Intent to educate her at home."

Mom adjusted her purse on her shoulder and gave a tight nod. "Okay, then. We'll give you a letter. And you'll get the notice in ten days."

"So, you think that's calendar days or business days?" she asked Dad a minute later as we hurried to the car. They were both looking kind of pale. "Because if it's business days that's really two weeks from today, but if—"

"No clue," Dad said. "But we're not just sending this letter in right away, okay? I want to give it a few weeks to see if he's right about private schools, or if this is really something we can handle."

Mom was nodding. "You're right. We could do, like, a two-week trial . . ."

My heart was so full I hardly listened. I didn't care if they called it a trial, or that they'd forgotten to call me Katya. They weren't sending me back. And I loved them for it.

By the time we got home I'd thought of the perfect way to thank them. I'd go on a foraging hike, find edible stuff in the woods, and make them a foraged-food feast.

Finding the recipes was no problem. The Internet was loaded with them. Chickweed pesto pizza, sumac lemonade, knotweed pie, acorn pancakes, pecan penuche. I had no clue what penuche was, and pecans didn't grow around here, but the rest sounded not only fun, but possible. I also found instructions for rose hip wine, red clover wine, dandelion wine, and elderberry wine, not to mention wild grape wine. And chopped ladies' thumb salad? Had to have that!

Mom had left me a list of chores, but since she had clients till six thirty, I stuck the journal in my backpack, along with my Swiss Army knife, Dad's trowel, some plastic bags, the wild foods websites I'd printed, and lunch, and headed out.

"No school today?" the mail carrier slowed to ask me as she passed.

My heart swelled. "Not for me!"

I picked a giant bunch of goldenrod, then climbed over

the stone wall for some purple asters, and chicory the color of the sky, and Queen Anne's lace. I could already see my bouquet on the table, surrounded by bowls and platters of strange-looking but hopefully delicious concoctions.

And here was my first find: a patch of ladies' thumb, growing in the ditch! I'd just begun filling a bag with the tiny pink flower-topped stems when a green minivan pulled up beside me.

"What are you doing out walking in the middle of the day?" Crissy Meehan, from next door, asked. "Didn't school start yesterday?"

My heart surged again. "I don't go to school anymore. I'm homeschooling."

"Oh, wow," she said. "Does that mean you can babysit in the day? Because I have a doctor's appointment tomorrow and I would so love not to bring the kids. It'd just be for, like, a few hours."

So not only was I free of school, I could also earn more money! "Sure," I said.

I was about to cross onto Great Hill Road, when Adele Williams's ancient blue station wagon slowed to pull into her driveway.

"Kaity, dear," she called in her rusty old-lady voice. "You wouldn't have a minute to help me, would you? I just bought some mums, and they're a little heavy for me to carry." She leaned across and opened the passenger door and I got in. She waited for me to buckle up before she started to drive, then said, "You're not at school."

"No!" The joy of saying it hadn't dulled a bit. "I'm home-schooling. And by the way, I've changed my name to Katya."

"Homeschooling?" The car almost went into the ditch as she turned to look at me. "I wouldn't have thought your family was the type for homeschooling."

"We are," I said.

"And you've finished your studies for the day so early?"

"Uh-uh. I'm looking for wild foods to make for dinner."

"What fun! My son used to love foraging with the Scouts. They didn't teach anything like that at school back then."

"They still don't," I said.

"So is this a homeschooling assignment?"

"Yep! Assigned by me!"

"Well, I've always thought that makes for the best sort of learning." She steered into the garage, narrowly missing taking off the mirror.

As I carried the chrysanthemums around to her patio I spotted an overgrown barberry bush, loaded with bright red berries. "Could I take some of your barberries?" I asked, having just read that you could actually eat barberries as well as put them in make-believe crumpets.

"Be my guest," she said. "Just mind the thorns." She smiled at me. "You know, it's so refreshing to see a young person so enthusiastic. So many of the kids these days—"

"I know!" I nodded. "Thank you."

I managed to pick a bagful without stabbing myself too badly. When I finished, I found that she'd wrapped my wildflower bouquet in wet newspaper and stuck it in a plastic shopping bag. Beside it on the porch step was a book. *Edible Wild Plants.*

"It has a recipe for barberry ketchup," she said. "We didn't think much of it, as I recall, but I believe the pickled milkweed pods were fairly tasty."

After thanking her again, and promising to bring her some of each, I cut through the woods behind her house to Alvin's field, where I found not just milkweed pods, but also, at the boggy back corner, jewelweed seeds, and a bunch of other plants I'd read about. Then, since I knew Dad would love making wine with me, I headed for the old hedgerow oak where Sean broke his tooth swinging on the grape vines. Along with grape vines, the tree seemed to have a lot of poison ivy, but I was careful, and, by standing on the stone wall, managed to pull down several fat bunches of grapes. Not enough for wine, but plenty for sugar-frosted grapes, which seemed like a great idea. Especially because the grapes didn't taste that good. I stuck them in my pack, then filled another bag with acorns.

Unbelievable! Eight things already—nuts, berries, greens, and fruit! No tubers, though. Dimitri was always going on about the nutritiousness of tubers.

1:10 p.m.
I don't miss having people around AT ALL.
I am fine with being by myself. I totally enjoy my own company.

While I ate the lunch I'd packed, I browsed through Mrs. Williams's book for tubers, and immediately spotted something I was sure grew in the ponds around here—arrowhead. But who knew that the roots could be boiled like potatoes, or roasted in ashes; that they were eaten year-round with meat and fish by Native Americans across the continent; that the squaws waded out into the water, then used their toes to dig the roots out of the mud; and that it was called wappatoo? Till just now, I wasn't even sure what a tuber was!

The path to Padgett's Pond was so overgrown that my clothes were covered with burrs by the time I got there. This end of the pond seemed to have turned into a swamp since I'd been here. But sure enough, there was my arrowhead—huge drifts of glossy, roundish leaves, with the arrow-shaped leaves sticking straight up, and the purplish flowers—exactly like the picture! How to get out to it, though? The water looked shallow, but there was no way to tell for sure.

Two ducks flapped off quacking as I approached. A turtle slipped off a log into the water.

Dear God, I prayed as I followed the shoreline. *Let there not be snapping turtles. Or snakes, or quicksand.*

What I needed was to find a canoe hidden in one of the brushy coves, or some fisherman's rowboat. I didn't see one. What I did find, in a shallowish-looking place, lying with one end on the shore and the other sticking into the water, was a forty-foot-long dead tree. It wouldn't get me all the way out to the arrowhead, but almost. Now if I could find a long forked stick, and walk out to the end of the log, I could try to snag some stems and yank the roots loose. I could already picture the bowl of roasted (boiled? French fried?) tubers on our table, with the card I'd make propped in front of it: WAPPATOO. NEVER OUT OF SEASON. GOOD WITH MEAT OR FISH. THERE'S ALWAYS ROOM FOR WAPPATOO.

Finding a perfect stick only took a minute. I parked my backpack, which was fairly heavy now, on a rock, along with the bag of wildflowers, and stepped onto the log. It was wide enough to walk on easily, and not slippery. The water was so clear, I could see minnows darting. About halfway to the end, though, the log got kind of narrow. I considered sitting and sliding to the end, or crawling along on my belly. I was debating how to sit down without spearing myself on one of the branch stubs, or getting my feet wet, when I saw, swimming out of the drifting arrowhead leaves, its pointy little head sticking up above the surface, its beady eyes aimed right at me as it slithered through the water directly toward my log, a long, thick, water snake.

I screamed. And in my scramble to turn around and get away, lost my balance. A nasty smell rose up as my feet sank into the yuck. The water went black and cloudy. Heart pounding, praying my shriek had scared the snake away, and that the other hundred snakes who clearly lived in the wappatoo weren't coming after me, and that I could pull my feet free of the mud and leaves, I splashed, fast as I could go, to land.

50

My jeans were wet up to my thighs. My sneakers were black and slimy. I sat on the shore end of the log and dumped the sludgy water out of them and cursed myself. Rosie would never be afraid of snakes. Rosie would have come home with a bag of wappatoo.

But as I picked my way back through the reeds and thistles to the field, I came across a little stream feeding into the pond, and, growing along its edges, a small, dark green leafy plant that looked just like the watercress in Stop & Shop. Since I was already wet, I waded in and tried a leaf. Definitely watercress. I picked a big bunch and stuck it in a plastic bag. A few minutes later I came across a sumac grove and, with my knife, hacked off some large clusters of the furry red berries, which, I knew from camp, made a really good lemonadey drink. Then, as I headed into the field, I found a wild apple tree with ugly but not-too-bitter apples, and some yellow, shriveled-looking but not-bad-tasting things that looked like plums.

So I had twelve things now—enough for a respectable feast even with no tubers.

2:30 In my quest for the famous wappatoo, I have just had an encounter with an immense and possibly poisonous water snake.
TO DO
—Read more about Native American foods (check if "squaw" is ethnic slur).
—Come up with wappatoo Plan B.

I was sitting eating one of the ugly apples, thinking about whether I'd tell Mom and Dad what had happened, when, from up at the top of Alvin's field, I heard the same weird sounds I'd heard last night. The part of me that had just recovered from the snake event told me to turn around and go home and start soaking my acorns. Instead, I crossed to where the field met the woods and, being careful to stay out of sight, worked my way up the hill through the brush.

On the rock, gazing out over the fields with a hideous scowl as he drew the hoarse, strangled-sounding screams from his violin, stood not a wild-eyed hermit but a tall boy in patchwork pajamas.

He stopped playing. "There's no point hiding in the bushes," he said. "I saw you coming."

So I stepped out. He was older than me. By how much I couldn't tell. His eyes were dark and round, his skin pale. His hair was a nice, glossy sort of horsey-brown, but it looked like someone had started to cut one side with nail scissors and then quit. The pajamas looked like they'd been made by the same person who cut his hair.

"Sorry," I said. "You don't have to stop because of me." Then, because I couldn't think what else to say, I added, "You play really well."

He looked at me as if I were the insane one. Which, I suddenly realized, I probably seemed like, with my scratched-up arms, burr-encrusted shirt, and mud-streaked, sodden jeans.

I pulled a stick out of my hair. "I was foraging," I said. "For wappatoo. It's an edible tuber. That grows in water."

"So I see," he said.

We stood there, me picking at the burdock burrs, him holding his violin and practically tapping his foot, waiting for me to go away.

My cell phone buzzed. I pulled it out of my pocket. It was a text message from Alyssa.

wassup k???? every1 is saying u think ur 2 kewl 4 skool. ive been telling them its not true but no 1s heard from u not even me. ru ok?

I hit SAVE and put the phone back.

"So, do you come here often?" I asked the boy. Oh, no! That sounded like I was trying to pick him up! I quickly added, "I mean to, you know . . . play?"

"Only when I'm in a really foul mood," he said.

"Well," I said. "Guess I'll be going."

He put his violin in its case. I turned to leave.

"Wait," he said.

I stopped. "What?" Was he going to walk with me? Did I want him to? Could he be a homeschooler too? "Were you going to ask why I'm not in school?" I said. "Because I don't go to school anymore. I'm homeschooling. As of today."

He raised his eyebrow. "Lucky you."

"No, no," I said. "I love it. I'm foraging food to make a foraged feast for my family."

His eyebrow went up again. "Peter Piper picked a peck of pickled peppers."

"Huh?"

"You had six *F*s in that sentence. I just noticed, that's all."

The conversation came to a stop again.

"Well, bye," I said. "I have fiddlehead ferns to find and fix." Then, for some reason, I reached into my backpack and pulled out the bag of grapes. "Want a grape?"

"Why not?" he said, taking a whole bunch. Then, wonder of wonders, as I turned to go, I saw him crack a smile.

📱 no, i am not *2 kewl 4 skool*!!! And i am
totally ok. i've only been homeschooling 1 day
and already been chased by a giant snake and met a
mystery boy. HS is the best thing EVER!

It felt so great not to worry about coolness anymore.

As soon as I got home, I sent the same message—minus the giant snake part, which I doubted anyone but my brother Sean would appreciate—to everyone else, including Francesca Halloran, since the best way to get news out at school was to tell the queen of the school. Then I e-mailed Dimitri, who answered in like five minutes.

✉ Hey, Katya, I'm excited to hear about your foraged
feast. I have not heard of wappatoo, but I am glad
you didn't get any. Unless water has been tested and
certified safe, you should not eat anything that grows
in it. So please do not eat that watercress. If it "looked
sort of like a plum and tasted sort of like a plum," it
was probably a plum, but next time, Katya, PLEASE

do not eat things unless you are sure exactly what they are! If you are really going to do this, you should find someone experienced to go out foraging with and help you with preparing. I do not mean to be a *wet blanket* but . . .

Mom wasn't altogether happy about the menu either. "I'm gonna take enough abuse for pulling you out of school," she said. "I don't need my father saying we're feeding him strange weeds." Because, as happened several times a week, Grandpa and his girlfriend, Cookie, had invited themselves to come over and bring dinner.

Dinnerwise, at least, that wasn't a bad thing, since the acorns and milkweed, not to mention the wine, turned out to take hours or days to prepare. Also, after an afternoon in my backpack, some of the leafier items didn't look that appealing. The chickweed cleaned up into a respectably fluffy-looking salad, though, and I made three kinds of drinks, and, for dessert, sugar-frosted grapes, which Mom thought might work on ice cream. And she said my wildflower bouquet looked gorgeous on the table.

Meanwhile the replies were coming in:

✉ **Rosie**: Sounds like ur *unschooling* like me. here's a great article about it. (attachment)
✉ **My brother Sean**: are you sure you know what you're getting into?
✉ **My other brother, Tommy**: Is this a good idea?

MVB's a pretty good place, even if it doesn't feel like that to you now.

✉ **Alyssa**: boy: kewl! snake: eeeeeeeewwww!

✉ **Jessie**: have you talked to Lindsey??????

✉ **Tyler**: if ur really not coming back do u mind if I ask out Linzy?

And then Grandpa and Cookie were here. So I answered only Tyler (knock yourself out) and my brothers (Yes!!).

"What'd you say this stuff was? Sumac juice?" Grandpa asked as I poured everyone a glass of the pale pink, actually pretty good-tasting drink. We were sitting around the porch table while we waited for dinner to heat up. He gave Cookie a wink. "I thought sumac was poisonous."

"Not unless it's poison sumac," I said.

I'm used to Grandpa messing with me, but Mom rolled her eyes at Dad and said, "Don't start, Pop."

"As you can see," I told Grandpa, pointing out the extremely cute info cards I'd written up, complete with preparation instructions, "we also have hot birch twig tea, and iced sweet fern tea. But I recommend the sumac lemonade."

"You do, do you?" Grandpa took his cigar out of his mouth and cut himself a hunk of cheese. He used to actually smoke the cigars till he met Cookie. These days he just kept one in his mouth and chewed on it till Cookie told him it was disgusting and he threw it out.

Cookie took a cautious sip, then gave me a thumbs-up.

"Mmm, nice and tart. Go ahead, try it, Anthony." Cookie has this sort of chirping voice that reminds me of a preK teacher. "So, is this like a nature study project you're doing for school, Kaity, honey?"

"Katya," Dad corrected her. "She'd like us to start calling her Katya."

"So, Katya," Grandpa said with an indulgent smile. "How's school going?" He was clearly avoiding his sumac lemonade. "What are you taking this year besides this nature stuff?"

"Well, actually . . ." I threw Mom a *What now?* look. She seemed almost as tense as in Westenburg's office.

"If you don't want the sumac, Pop," she told him, "I'll go get you some wine. But I think it's very refreshing, don't you, Joe?" She took a big, loyal swig.

Dad did too. Then he poured himself some sweet fern tea, swirled it around in his glass, stuck his nose in the glass, and sniffed. "Hmm . . ." He put on a pursed-lip wine critic face and a snooty accent. "I'm picking up a hint of mint, a nice herbaceous tang, and a long, ferny finish."

I rolled my eyes at him.

"No," he said. "I'm serious. It's good. Who'd of thunk it? The only question is"—he gave Cookie a smile—"which goes best with stuffed shells?"

Mom jumped to her feet. "I'll check if they're heated through."

He stood up. "I'll come with you and dress Kai . . . Katya's salad."

"I'll help!" I said. "Back in a minute, Grandpa. You're not leaving me alone to tell him?" I said as I rushed after them to the kitchen.

"No," Dad said. "I was just thinking he'll take it better on a full stomach. Go talk to Cookie about chickweed or something."

"Chickweed, a common plant of lawns and gardens," I read off the info card when I got back to the table. "Mild and tasty in salad. Excellent source of vitamins and minerals. Also good for cuts and rashes."

"Does it work on athlete's foot?" Grandpa leaned down as if to untie his shoe. "That might be better than eating it."

"Anthony!" Cookie gave him a smack. "I bet it's delicious. Plus, you can weed the lawn and make dinner at the same time." She turned to me again. "I hope you washed it."

"Of course she washed it." Mom came out with the enormous foil pan of pasta. "It happens to look very appetizing too. There's nothing wrong with trying something new for a change. Change can be good, right, Joe?" She threw Dad a look like, *Okay. You can take it from here.*

"Shall we eat our salad first?" Dad set the big wooden salad bowl in the middle of the table and, with that two spoons in one hand thing I can never do, piled salad into each of our bowls.

Chickweed looks like no lettuce you've ever seen. It's also not crunchy like lettuce. But with Dad's olive oil and wine vinegar, it did make a tasty salad. I forked up a giant mouthful.

"You gonna eat some, Grandpa?"

"I'll let Cookie be the guinea pig," he said. "If she don't keel over, I'll give it a try. Or"—he looked around—"where's Waffle?"

Cookie gave him another smack. "Cut it out, Anthony. What are these cute little pieces of flower in it, Kaity sweetie?"

I couldn't resist. "Chopped ladies' thumbs."

"Oh, yeah?" Grandpa said. "So what'd you do with the rest of the ladies?"

I'd bet Dad five dollars he'd say that. Dad had refused to take the bet.

"Or are we having them for dessert?" Grandpa poked Cookie, who'd begun serving out giant portions of pasta. "Get it? Lady fingers?"

"Don't be so quick to mock," she said, grating some extra cheese on his shells before passing him his plate. "I wish I'd learned something this useful in school," she said as she passed me mine. "In my day, all we had was home ec. Like I really needed to go to school to learn to boil an egg."

"This is what I'm saying!" I said. By now everyone had eaten up their salad, including Grandpa, who'd polished off every last leaf. "Grandpa, bet you didn't know you can use the thorns from hawthorn trees for fishhooks. And to open cans if you're camping. And I'm sure there are plants that'd cure athlete's foot—"

"Ahem!" Dad cleared his throat. "Speaking of not learning things at school . . ." He looked at Mom like, *Back to you.*

"We're not totally sure Kaitlyn will be in school this year," Mom said.

"Why? What's the matter?" Grandpa's worried eyes went to my face. "Is she sick? What's going on?"

"I'm fine," I said. "I'm just—"

"We're just not sure Martin Van Buren's the best place for her," Mom finished for me.

Grandpa put his fork down. "What are you talking about? Since when? She's on the honor roll, she gets to go to all the games with band—"

"We're probably gonna look into some private schools," Dad said. "But we're also thinking about—"

"Private school?" Grandpa said. "Don't private schools cost like thirty grand a year—"

"I know," Dad said. "We haven't decided anything yet. We're just looking at our options."

"What's wrong with Immaculate Heart?" Cookie said. "I sent my kids there. Immaculate Heart's a good school."

Dad threw me a *Stay out of this!* look and nodded diplomatically. "That's definitely something else to think about."

"We've got a couple different options," Mom said. "One of them's homeschooling."

"Which," I said, "I've already—"

"Homeschooling? Are you out of your mind?" Grandpa glared from one to the other of us. "Donna, don't tell me this was your idea? Joe, you went along with this? You haven't joined one of them . . . movements without telling me?" I could almost see a light go on in his brain. "Is that

61

why she's got the new name, and we're eating all this back-to-nature—"

"Anthony!" Cookie put her hand on his arm. "Kait . . . Katya went to a lot of trouble to make these dishes for you. Don't be rude! And whatever their reasons are, I'm sure they're good ones."

"Yeah, if you're a nut job or a fanatic. I know the schools aren't what they used to be, but homeschooling? Where would you even get a crazy, off-the-wall—"

Dad put up his hand. "Believe me, Pop, when Kai . . . Katya brought it up, I—"

"You're gonna listen to a thirteen-year-old? If she said she wanted to jump off the Brooklyn Bridge—"

"I know." Dad talked over him. "And I'm still not sold on it. But after going to school with her this morning and talking to the principal, Donna and I decided to give it a try for two weeks—"

"And who's gonna teach her?" Grandpa tipped his chin toward Mom. "You've never taught. You work in the salon all day. You haven't set foot in a school in twenty-five years. This is the worst idea I ever heard. It's a recipe for disaster."

"I'll have you know"—Mom's voice was stiff—"that I may not have been in school for twenty-five years, or be a teacher, but I happen to be a very good networker. I've already found out that there are quite a few homeschooling families in the area—"

"There are?" My mind jumped to Mystery Boy.

"And I have plenty of clients who are retired teachers,

who I'm sure would love to help me out in exchange for haircuts. And I've already arranged to talk to Mary Garvey's cousin, who teaches middle school over in Branford, about curriculum. *Plus* reserved all the homeschooling books from the library, *and* borrowed a blackboard—"

"And you know, I was a teacher," Cookie said. Grandpa shot her a dirty look, which she ignored. "Of course, that was third grade, but I'd be happy to work with her."

Blackboard? Curriculum? Cookie?

Mom must have read my mind. Her mouth tightened. "Homeschool is school. School has blackboards. And we can use all the help we can get. Thank you, Cookie."

Grandpa's ranting hadn't gotten to me at all. Now, suddenly, I felt like crying.

Cookie gave me a pat. "Shall we have a little dessert? You said you made us a dessert."

"I don't need dessert," Grandpa said. "Let's go home. It's time for our shows."

Mom started banging around the kitchen the minute they left. "Why do I even let him come over here?" she yelled as she rammed plates in the dishwasher. "He is just so ready to tell me what I am not able to do!" Her arm knocked into the pan of pasta. It dumped out onto the floor. She cursed.

"He's an old guy," Dad said, reaching for the paper towels. "With a short fuse. He just wants the best for Kaity."

"An old jerk is more like it! He did the same exact thing when I started the business, remember?"

I'd seen her yell at Grandpa a hundred times, but she never, ever badmouthed him in front of me.

"Listen," Dad said as he squatted down to clean up the mess. "You think he might be so upset about homeschooling, he'll cough up some money for private school? That'd solve this whole thing, wouldn't it?"

She snorted. "It'd be great. But I don't think he has it."

"He has it," Dad said. "So don't go getting him all hot and bothered. You know what I'm saying?"

I tried to keep my voice calm. "Why are you talking about private school? And solving this? It's solved. I'm doing this the way Rosie does. It's called unschooling. I'll show you the article. When you unschool, all of life is your school. The world is your classroom. You decide what your interests are and then you follow them, wherever they take you."

Mom stopped wiping down the counter. "Oh, really."

"Yeah," I said. "So tomorrow morning I'm gonna go see if Mrs. Williams has any more books I can borrow, and then go out— "

"No," she said. "Tomorrow morning—" The phone rang. She picked it up and listened, frowning. "No, I'm sorry Crissy. . . . Yes, I know, but she won't be free during the day. I'm sure she'd be happy to babysit any evening, though." She hung up and turned back to me. "Tomorrow morning we're figuring out how you can help in the salon. So we'll know if I can free up enough time to work with you. Another thing I did this afternoon," she told Dad, "was check the state requirements for manicurists. I didn't see anything that said you had to be a certain age. So I'm going to start showing her the basics."

"Of doing nails?" I was at the edge of shouting.

"You knew we were gonna have to work together on this!" she said. "It can't be a total shock that I can't just drop everything to accommodate you."

"I'm not asking you to!" I said. "I don't need you to!"

She turned to Dad. "And Joe, I'm thinking you'll need to build her a desk in the corner of the salon. I can always turn it into a manicure station if this doesn't work out."

"Right!" I was totally shouting now. "And I can do Ms. Pinchbeck's nails while Cookie teaches me!"

"Hey!" She whirled to face me. "Don't go getting all pissed off at me! I'm not the one who came up with this home-schooling idea. You said you needed to do it, so I'm trying to do it. I've already taken enough crap from Grandpa. I don't need a hard time from you too!"

I had that feeling in my stomach that you get when you know the other person's right, and that you have no business wanting to kill them, so then you feel like a terrible person, which makes you even madder.

I had to swallow hard to say it, but I did. "Okay."

CHAPTER 9

She woke me at six the next morning. "We've got a very full day today," she said. "It's the hairspray crowd, so I don't want you to wear those ratty jeans."

There's a dress code for homeschooling? I thought of saying. But she still looked pretty tightly wound, so I kept my mouth shut and put on the jeans without holes, and tried not to tune out as she gave me a quick bio of each customer, and whether they'd booked a perm or cut or color, and what I could do to assist.

Answer the phone, it turned out. "A Cut Above. Good morning, this is Katya." Ask if they'd like a cup of coffee, and make sure they had a magazine to read under the dryer, and sweep up the hair when they were done, and smile agreeably when they said things like "I love your new assistant, Donna." Also, throw yesterday's smocks in the washing machine, fold the towels, delete duplicate client—"Not customers! We don't call them customers!"—records from the computer, and count how many bottles of volumizer were left, then call to order more.

Except for the poison ivy, I'd have thought yesterday's

freedom was a dream. It started in the night, with a few blisters on my ankle. By the time Mom woke me, I had another whole itchy line of them on my arm. By mid-morning, I felt like one big raging itch.

"Don't scratch! You'll spread it! And don't let the clients see it!" Mom scolded each time she could say it without one of them hearing. Which was hard, because they were acting like I was the most interesting thing they'd seen in years. Everyone seemed to know somebody who knew somebody over in somewhere-or-other who either homeschooled or knew about it. Nobody said anything negative, probably because they were afraid Mom would take it out on their hair.

DAY 3 OF MY NEW LIFE
I can't believe it's still only 11 o'clock! I hate the smell in here.

Between clients, Mom read homeschool websites and worked on her supply list:

- *Printer paper*
- *Whiteboard*
- *Week at a glance calendar*
- *Lesson plan book*
- *Magic Markers*

At lunchtime, Cookie arrived. "Don't buy the lesson plan book," she said. "I've got one for you. Red pencils too, a whole box, brand-new." She opened a bottle of hair gel, gave it a sniff, then poured a little in her hand. "I was also thinking, Donna . . ." She walked over to the mirror and rubbed the product through her hair. "Unless you have another idea for PE, she could come to my hip-hop aerobics class. Also, I meant it last night about the teaching. Not to boast, but I'm very good at math. What math is she doing this year?"

"Algebra." Mom's eyes narrowed. "But what's Pop gonna say about all that?"

Cookie shrugged. "He'll have to deal with it."

No, he won't, I thought. *Because it's not happening. None of it's happening.* But I didn't say it. And didn't plan to, at least not till we were safely through the trial.

1:30 p.m.
Two weeks of this? Can you die of poison ivy??????

Over the summer Mom had installed one of those fancy massage-action pedicure chairs. Before "our" two thirty arrived, she explained the difference between a regular pedicure and a spa pedicure and showed me how the foot spa worked, and how to wind that little cotton strip between a client's toes.

"Just promise me you're not gonna make me touch some old lady's feet, okay?" I said.

"It's not an old lady," Mom said. "Mr. Horton's a real

sweetie. I'm sure he won't mind if I demonstrate a few of
the basics on him for you."

2:15 p.m.
Arrrrgh!!!!!!!

While waiting for Mr. Horton, I discovered that if I sat
backward on the pedicure chair, pretzeling my legs so the
one with the poison ivy was on top of the butt massager,
and turned the massage action to high, the chair became a
Scratchomatic. Oh, the relief! I felt like rolling around and
waving my legs in the air, like Waffle. While I massaged
my itches, I checked my phone for messages. Nothing.
But that wasn't surprising, since I hadn't answered anyone,
and probably good, since I wasn't exactly eager to tell them
that my amazing new life had taken a sudden turn for the
worse.

"Get offa there!" Mom whispered as Mr. Horton walked
in the door. "Eddie, I'd like you to meet my daughter,
Kait . . . Katya."

Mr. Horton didn't look like how I pictured a man who
came for weekly pedicures. He looked more like he'd be sitting on the stool next to Grandpa at the Dutch Treat.

"Take your time, take your time," he said as I unfolded
my legs and jumped down. "I'm not moving too fast today."
He walked stiffly to the chair. "Looks like you've got a little
poison ivy there."

"She got it in the woods out by you," Mom said, wiping

the chair down before helping him climb onto it. Then she sat on the low stool in front of him, and, while she un-Velcroed his shoes and pried them off his feet, told him about my foraging. "But we didn't get to eat most of it." She made a wry face. "My dad came over."

Mr. Horton laughed. "He don't exactly strike me as the wild foods type, your dad. Did you try rubbing jewelweed on her poison ivy?"

"Jewelweed?" Why I hadn't heard about that at camp? "Jewelweed cures poison ivy?"

"Oh, yeah!" he said. "You just crush the stems and make sure you rub the juice on real good. It'll help them mosquito bites on your neck too."

"Cool!" I said. "I know exactly where to find some!"

Mom was right. I did like Mr. Horton.

She motioned me to come over and sit on the floor next to her, then picked up his leg so I could see his foot. "How's it look to you?"

"Okay, I guess," I said, not wanting to look too closely.

"You guess or you're sure?" she said. "This is important. Mr. Horton has diabetes. That's why he comes here every week. We're looking for any breaks in the skin, or red spots, or signs of trouble with his circulation. Then, after we make sure everything's okay, we wash each foot and dry it very thoroughly."

Mr. Horton looked embarrassed. "If I could reach 'em myself, or see the bottoms, I'd spare your mom the bother."

"Excuse me," Mom said. "If it's not a bother painting someone's toes pink, it's not a bother to keep your feet healthy. Plus, we're homeschooling. This counts as education."

"Thank you, Donna," he said. "I appreciate that. Just be warned, Katya. They're not a pretty sight."

They sure weren't.

We had one more client after that. Then Mom went off to town, I grabbed my books and notebook, and I was outta there!

As soon as I got close to Alvin's field, I strained my ears for Mystery Boy's violin. All I heard was a distant lawn mower. Even so, I could feel my spirits lifting. Hey, if I'd escaped from school, I could get out of algebra. And maybe it was wishful thinking, but when I rubbed the jewelweed juice on the poison ivy, it helped the itches instantly.

I wondered if it worked on zits too.

ANOTHER PROJECT IDEA: MEDICINAL HERBS
1. Find out everything that grows around here that the Native Americans used for healing.
2. Start collecting!
3. Use Mom's database program for plant inventory??
4. Find out if jewelweed works on fungus-y things like athlete's foot—try an experiment on Grandpa???

It was amazing how fast the time passed when I was outside!

Dad was just coming in the door when I got home.

"So I printed out the state's homeschool rules," Mom told him even before he'd greeted Waffle. Her mood seemed to have picked up as much as mine. "Listen to this!" She grabbed a sheet of paper from the pile on the counter. "'Teacher qualifications: None! Testing requirement: None!'"

I dropped my backpack on the counter. "Perfect!"

"Yeah, this says all we have to do, after we withdraw and file our Notice of Intent—which you don't really have to, but Westenburg said do it, so we'll do it—is teach the required subjects, and be able to show that you're getting equivalent instruction in the studies taught in the public schools."

"Not a problem," I said, thinking of all I'd accomplished in the past two hours. "It'll be better than the public schools. A hundred times better."

"That's what I'm hoping," Mom said. "I just took out every homeschooling book in the library. And when I went on the Internet, Joe, I got one million seven hundred eighty thousand hits for eighth-grade lesson plans. Do you believe that? Plus, teacher guides for every subject. They even show you how to set up an instruction matrix."

"Whoa! Slow down, ladies," Dad said. "And here I was thinking we'd spend tonight looking up private schools."

"We still can," Mom said. "But I read that without all the wasted time at school, most homeschooled kids do their lessons in like three or four hours. So if Katya takes over the clerical and housekeeping-type jobs for me—see, I remembered to call you Katya this time—I'll have a couple of good hours in the mornings to work with her. Then, if I review her work over lunch, and jump in during the day as needed . . ."

"That still sounds like a lot of time out of your day," Dad said. "It'll shake up your whole routine . . ."

She gave him a long look. "I might be ready to shake things up a little."

"Well," he said. "It'd be a lot more affordable than private school. What do you say, Kaity? Are you ready to work with Mom and Cookie?"

The way he said Cookie's name made me think he knew the answer. It was all I could do not to blurt out that we didn't need teacher guides and lesson plans. That my own plans could keep me busy for weeks, maybe months. I had to remind myself to be grateful we were doing this at all, and that if I went along and bided my time . . .

I nodded.

"Okay, then. Here's the deal." He took off his glasses and gave me a long, eyebrow-bunched look. "Number one, we need to make sure you're not falling behind."

Behind what? I thought of saying. *That's the whole point. There is no behind anymore.*

I kept my mouth shut.

"Second, it can't put too much of a strain on Mom. This has to work for both of you. If it doesn't work for Mom, it doesn't work."

DAILY INSTRUCTIONAL MATRIX

Lesson Time	Required Subjects	Instruction
8–8:45	U.S. History Geography Citizenship	with Mom
9–9:45	Writing Spelling Grammar	
10–10:45	Math	with Cookie
11–3	K works on own Lunch K assists in Salon	with Mom or independently

✉ To: Dimitri Olshansky
Subject: Question
Hey, Dimitri, do you see a good reason why I need to study algebra?

✉ To: Katya
Subject: Answer
Yes. To be a scientist you need math.

✉ To: Dimitri Olshansky
Subject: RE: Answer
Well, does learning Quickbooks so I can do my mom's
bookkeeping for her count as math?????

✉ To: Katya
Subject: RE: Answer
Uh . . . I'm not touching that! Just remember, it's all
education.

✉ To: Dimitri Olshansky
Subject: Yes, well
What about learning to do online bill payments? And
learning to mix up hair colors? Did I mention she got
one million seven hundred thousand hits for eighth-
grade lesson plans? I think she's downloaded all of
them. This stuff is taking me all day. I have no time for
my own stuff.

✉ To: Katya
Subject: So . . .
do your own stuff afterward.

In other words, stop whining.

He was right, of course. The next day when I got done
in the salon I thought about working on my own projects.
But by then I felt like I'd earned a little break, and before I
knew it, it was midnight.

Day 4
Sunday
Spent all yesterday and today helping
D make the desk. Fun, I guess, but it
meant I didn't get out at all this weekend
except for church and lunch at Aunt Angie's,
who is almost as rabidly anti-homeschooling
as Grandpa.

Day 6
Tues.
Thought maybe Mom would ease off after
a few days, but no. She told Aunt A and
G all the wonderfully educational things
"we're" doing, so now "we" have to do
them. FIVE HOURS at the desk today.

5 p.m.
Okay I know I'm whining, but Quickbooks
sucks. I hate tutorials. I have no interest
in the history of Connecticut. I loathe,
detest, and despise algebra. Why am I still
doing worksheets? Why aren't we doing
science?????

Day 7
Wed
2 p.m.
She and Cookie are liking teaching WAY too much! I don't care that they're being nice. I've created a couple of monsters!

4 p.m.
Told her this is school all over again, except with the smell of hairspray. Didn't mean to say it, it just slipped out. Loud. She told me to remember our deal. Said I was sorry (a lie) and told her, amazingly nicely, I thought, that it's because I haven't been outside more than 1 hr a day in a week. She suggested we join a homeschool group together so I could have some "outside activities." I said that wasn't what I meant by outside. Said I'd rather do hip-hop aerobics. She totally didn't get that I was being sarcastic!

I thought my brothers might take my side. They're big outdoors/don't-make-me-sit-at-a-desk-ever types. It's why they work construction in Maine. "She hovers!" I told them. "She wants to know what I'm doing, and how I'm doing, and if I'm done yet."

They both said basically the same thing: Tried to warn

you. Good thing this is just a trial. School's gonna look really good when you get back.

I thought about calling Rosie then. But she'd kind of warned me too.

12:40 a.m.
Am I being an ungrateful wretch????
2:45 a.m.
Dear . . . who?????
I have this thing I want to do with my life.
I know how pompous and corny it sounds
to say I feel it in my heart, but I do. I
know it's right for me. And I know that if
I'm patient, I can make it happen. I'm just
not sure I can stand another week in the
salon.

I did it, though. I stayed from eight each morning till at least three each afternoon. I didn't call the Daily Instructional Matrix, staring down at me from the whiteboard, The Dim. I trudged through the worksheets and wrote my essays and sat through my algebra lessons, and posted the bill payments, and prepped clients, and messed with my hair a lot, and didn't even think about discovering anything till Thursday afternoon, when Mr. Horton asked if the jewelweed worked, and I realized I'd put my brain on hold so totally, I'd forgotten about the jewelweed and the poison ivy.

The minute his feet were washed and his shoes back on, I told Mom, "I'm outta here."

I was almost to the door when the phone rang.

"Could you get that?" she called.

I groaned and came back.

"Good afternoon. A Cut Above."

I hated this dippy greeting.

"Kaity?" It was Grandpa, sounding crabby.

I handed Mom the phone.

"I'll be right with you," she told the client who had just

arrived. "Sweetie, before you leave, would you get Mrs. Lowenstein a robe and bring her some tea or coffee? We're fine," she told Grandpa. "No, what article? What'd it say?"

Mrs. Lowenstein was looking me up and down. "Do you have any herbal tea? Not one of the Zingers, though. I don't like the Zingers."

"We have chamomile," I said.

"Yeah, I know what unschooling is," Mom told Grandpa. Rolling her eyes in apology to Mrs. Lowenstein and mouthing, "This'll just take a minute," she stepped out onto the landing. She'd lowered her voice, but I could still hear her through the screen door as I rummaged through the tea bag jar. "No, Pop. Don't worry. We're not unschooling. Believe me. That's not what we're doing here."

Not yet, I thought. In the half hour since deciding to go out to the woods, I'd had three new project ideas. All good. And starting Monday, when the letter went in . . .

"She's not falling behind, Pop. Trust me. Or ask Cookie. Who is doing a fantastic job with Kaity, by the way."

"You know, I'm going to pass on the tea," Mrs. Lowenstein said as I brought her the cup. "I'm kind of in a rush."

"Me too," I told her. I needed to run in and get the camera and the plant books, so I could start the medicinal plant inventory. And I knew it was ridiculous to think Mystery Boy would be on Alvin's field again, but I hadn't seen anyone under the age of forty in a week.

"Yeah. Algebra. . . ." Mom's voice rose. "What? She didn't tell you?"

And now she was lighting a cigarette. Not a good sign.

"In fact, I'm not going to bother changing," Mrs. Lowenstein said. "I have a meeting with my lawyer at four. Can we just get started?"

We?

"You can approve or disapprove, Pop," Mom was saying. "It doesn't give you the right . . ."

Mrs. Lowenstein looked me over again. "That is, if you know how."

Know how to hand you a robe and seat you at the shampoo basin? It's not rocket science, I felt like saying. I picked out a robe from the XL pile.

"Right this way," I said.

Mrs. Lowenstein had a big, curly mop of hair, the kind that fights back when you try to get it all into position in the basin. She also had a fat neck that didn't fit easily in the head slot, and a bulbous head.

"Careful!" She winced as I tried to shove her neck into position. "I left work early so I could get my hair cut before I see my lawyer. I can't be late."

I checked the landing. Mom was still talking. "I know. You said."

"Well, can you just get me washed, please?"

I looked again to see if Mom was coming. She wasn't. She was gonna owe me for this. Big-time.

"No problem."

I turned on the water and aimed the sprayer at Mrs. Lowenstein's hair.

"That's too hot!" she yelled. "Turn it down! You're burning me!"

Oops. I'd forgotten Mom's number one rule: Test the temperature. "Sorry. I'm so sorry." I tested the temperature, then gave her head a gentle squirt. "How's that?"

"Better," she said grudgingly.

So I pressed the sprayer all the way. But I must not have had her neck arranged right.

"It's running down my back!" she screamed. "This is a silk blouse. It water spots."

Then why didn't you change? I didn't say that. "I'm so sorry." I set the sprayer on the edge of the sink so I could grab a towel, but the minute I let go of it, the hose whipped around like a crazed snake, shooting water on the walls, on me, and all over Mrs. Lowenstein.

"What, are you trying to drown me?" she shrieked, struggling to sit up to escape the spray. I grabbed the hose and turned the water off, but not before she was totally drenched. "Do you know what you're doing at all?" she snapped, water running down her glasses.

With that sodden mop, she looked like a pissed-off sheep.

"What are you laughing at?" she demanded. "This is funny to you?"

It was more than funny. It was the only good thing that had happened in more than a week.

"Donna!" she bellowed as I handed her a towel. "You'd better get in here. Now!"

"Even you have to admit she looked funny," I told Mom after she'd made me apologize about six more times, and she'd cut Mrs. Lowenstein's hair for free.

"I don't care how funny she looked," Mom said. "She's a client. Who refers other clients. And she told me she didn't like your attitude."

"Didn't like my attitude? What about her attitude? And the way she talked at me, like I was her servant or something?"

I did finally get out to the woods after that. But I was too busy stomping around rehashing the whole stupid event to notice anything. Except that Mystery Boy wasn't there.

Mom was rehashing it to Dad when I got back. With still not a single speck of humor. And not a clue about my side.

I threw my pack down on the counter where they were making dinner. "I never asked to be her flunky, Dad! That was her idea, not mine. I don't even want to be up there in the salon with her. It used to be fun being around her. This isn't fun!"

"Yeah?" Mom ripped the skin off a chicken breast. "Well, I happen to be working just a little too hard at the moment for this to be fun!" She grabbed the mallet and started pounding out the chicken. "You think it's easy, planning out not just your entire day but your whole curriculum." *Wham! Wham!* "Grading your papers, reading your essays, worrying if I'm gonna screw it up, or miss something, and you'll fall behind?" *Wham!* She didn't look at me. "On top of running a business?" *Wham!* "With no one to tell me how to do this, and everyone, including your brothers, ready to tell me everything I'm doing wrong? Do you know how many hours I spend every night reading all these home-school books?"

"Then stop!" I yelled back. "Who asked you to? Let me stay in my room, where I won't screw things up for you and can do my own work, not your ridiculous daily instructional ma—!"

She whacked the chicken again. "It is not ridicu—"

"Enough!" Dad's eyes were scary dark. "If you don't like the way this is going, Kaity, we'll give it up right now. You can go back to school. Just get on the bus tomorrow morning. Honey"—he turned to Mom—"I'd say that chicken's flat enough."

I felt like a giant yawning hole had opened in my stomach. "Maybe I will," I said.

But as soon as I got to my room, I knew that if I was going to give this up, it was because I decided. Not because they told me to.

So I was back in the salon again the next morning.

"Good afternoon, I mean good morning. A Cut Above." I'd stopped bothering with the "Katya speaking."

"Good morning," a quavery old-lady voice on the other end said. "I'd like a liposuction please."

"I'm sorry," I said. "We don't do that here."

"But my butt is so big! It's out of control! You have to help me!" The voice dissolved into giggles. I heard other giggles too. "Do you do amputations? This is Aida Pinchbeck."

"Jessie!" I couldn't believe how happy I was to hear from her.

"We're just checking to see if you're still alive," she said. "No one's heard anything from you in a week."

"I know. Sorry." Mom looked up from grading my geography worksheet to see who I was talking to. "I'm fine."

"Yeah?" Jessie sounded like she didn't believe me.

I tried to put more conviction in my voice. "Yeah. Homeschooling is great. I really like it."

"And you're really working at your mom's salon?"

My stomach clenched. It would take about thirty seconds for the news to get around school if I admitted it, even if I told her to keep it quiet. "No, I'm . . . just, you know, up here . . . doing my own projects, working on the computer—"

"That's not what I heard!" she said. "The lady you nearly drowned yesterday? She's in my mom's Pilates class. She said you're the new assistant."

"Well, I'm not!" I said. "And even if I was"—I checked if Mom was listening—"it's gonna change. In fact"—I had only today to get through in the salon till we sent in the withdrawal letter—"I'm just trying to, like, suck it up until it does."

"Then you better hurry up and learn to cut hair," Jessie said. "So you can give us all free haircuts! Ouch! Hold on. Stop hitting me, Alyssa! I am not being mean! Get on the other phone if you want to talk to her."

"So you're not really there in the salon all day long?" Alyssa asked. "I mean, I like your mom and all, but how is that?"

How do you think? I smell like hair. When I'm not doing worksheets, I'm reading Modern Maturity *under the desk, and disinfecting the foot spa.*

"It's fine," I said.

"Sorry." Alyssa's voice was kind. "I knew there had to be something up. I knew you didn't just ditch us. So I guess homeschooling isn't the best thing ever, huh?"

I'd been praying they'd forgotten those gloating messages. "Not really."

"We miss you," she said. "Everyone here misses you."

"Except maybe Lindsey and Tyler," Jessie said. "Who we totally hate, by the way."

"I don't care about them," I said. I really didn't. My throat tightened. "I just wish I knew what to do."

"Well, you could always try spraying cold water down people's necks a few more times," Jessie said. "Or spilling peroxide on their heads. Or telling them their new hairstyle makes them look like crap."

"Have you, like, officially quit school?" Alyssa asked.

"No." I felt that yawning hole opening in my stomach again. "Not officially. Not yet." I lowered my voice so Mom wouldn't hear. "We don't have to decide for like four more days." The blood roared in my ears as I heard myself say the word *decide*.

"Okay," she said, "so you gave it your best shot and it sucked. So come back."

I didn't answer her.

"Well, one thing you should definitely do," Jessie said. "You should come to the dance tomorrow night."

Day 11
Friday
Dear . . . who???
I wish you could tell me what to do. oh, argh. Maybe the dance will tell me.

CHAPTER 11

The old familiar mac and cheese smell, as we walked through the front doors the next night, made my heart shrink. So then why were my nerves buzzing like this, and my heart pounding harder than the music?

"Well, your life may suck," Jessie said, giving my hair a last fluff as we neared the gym. "But your hair looks great. Is mine still okay?"

"It's fine. It's the same people we've seen every day of our lives, remember?" Why had I eaten Cookie's garlic bread with dinner? She'd also put a ton of garlic in the broccoli raab.

"You both look great," Alyssa said as I stuck another piece of gum in my mouth. "Don't worry, Kaity, we won't say anything about the beauty parlor. Do I have too much blush on?"

"No," I said. "It looks good. Do I?"

The gym had its usual corny autumn leaves decorations, and the usual knots of girls on one side, boys on the other. But the DJ was great. I could feel the thump of the bass from my throat down through my belly, all the way to my toes. And being around kids again, hearing them laughing and shouting, picking up the energy . . . I felt this surge of . . . was it just nerves, or was I happy to be back?

I grabbed Alyssa's and Jessie's arms. "Let's dance!"

"Let's talk to some people first!" Jessie shouted to be heard over the music.

From over at the refreshments table, my seventh-grade math teacher, Ms. McLaine, uncovered her ears to wave to me. She didn't look nearly as vicious as I remembered. In fact, she looked glad to see me. So did Mr. Zingarelli, amazingly.

"Here they come!" Alyssa shouted. "People! Boy people! Your fans!"

It was Matt Schmidt, with some short kid I didn't know. Matt had been my stand partner in band for two years, and never talked to me. Or anyone. "How's homeschooling?" he hollered.

If the news had trickled down to Matt, the whole school knew. I shrugged. "It's okay."

"No, it's not!" Jessie shouted.

"Well, we miss you in band," he said.

"You do?" I never practiced, came late to rehearsals . . .

"Yeah, no. We do." Even in this light I could see he was blushing. "You want to dance?"

"She's got some people to see," Jessie said before I could say "Yeah, okay." Matt had gotten cuter since last year. Or I'd stopped being so shallow. "Maybe later," she added.

"What people?" I asked as he walked away.

"Francesca!" she said. "She's over there with her girls, looking at you right now. Did you see her shoes? I saw them last week at Bloomie's—"

"Uh-oh!" Alyssa grabbed my arm. "Don't kill me, Kaity! I think I see—"

"Tyler?" I cursed. They'd sworn he wasn't going be here.

But there he was, walking in with Jack and Cody, all loose-limbed and baggy-jeaned and swagger-cool. No Lindsey, though, whatever that meant.

"Should we pretend we don't see him?" Alyssa asked.

Too late. They were headed right for us.

"Heyyyyy." He gave us that slow, lazy smile. "How's it goin'? How's life at home?"

"Crappy," Jessie said.

He pooched his lip out. "Bad move leaving us, huh?"

"That's what she's here to find out," Jessie said. "Where's Lindsey?"

He shrugged. "Dunno. But Kaity, if you ever need help deciding . . ."

I wouldn't ask you, I started to finish for him. But that sounded so lame and hokey. "In case you were wondering about your hat, I . . ."—buried it with a tuna sandwich sounded too much like I still cared—"stuck it in the mail."

Jess and Alyssa looked at me like, *Why don't we know about this?*

"But you might not get it for a while," I said. "I sent it fifth class."

That buzzy feeling was coming back.

90

"*Is* there a fifth class?" Francesca Halloran gave Tyler a dismissive "Hey" as she joined us.

"Yeah," I said. "It's for stuff you don't care about at all."

"That is so interesting that you're homeschooling, Kaity!" she shouted. "So is it, like, really depressing and horrible to come here and see us all?"

She looked beautiful tonight. Per usual. And coolly perfect.

"No! Homeschool sucks!" Jessie shouted back, as with a "Well, see ya around," Tyler and his friends drifted away. "Big mistake! We're trying to talk her into coming back. I love your shoes!"

"Really? Thanks." Francesca glanced from her black ballet flats to my new Birkenstocks—brown suede, like Rosie's—which I'd ordered online over Mom's *Ick!*s and *Yuck!*s. "Those look comfy," she shouted.

By which I'd have thought she meant hideous, except that she was looking me over like I was this new and interesting cool person.

I was totally buzzing now.

"So then *are* you thinking of coming back to school?" she asked.

My throat clenched. Admitting defeat to someone so perfectly perfect felt as impossible as telling Rosie.

"Actually," I said, "I like homeschooling."

"Really." Her clear blue eyes zeroed in on me. "What do you like about it?"

"Uh . . . that I'm not here?"

91

She laughed and nodded. "I know what you mean."

But I wished I'd said something more intelligent. I also didn't want my friends to think I was insulting them. "I like the freedom," I heard myself telling her. Which kind of surprised me, since I had none. But the song had ended, and Francesca looked so interested that I said, "I mean, I'm sure school is fine for some people. People who are fine with doing what they're told and following the rules and basically being sheep. But there are those of us who can't do that, who really have to make our own direction . . ."

"I know what you mean." She nodded again. "I'm such a people person, though. I'd go nuts by myself in my room all day."

"Not me," I said. "I'm fine being by myself. And I don't actually . . ."

The music had started up again, with a pounding beat that made it impossible to be heard. I half hoped Jessie and Alyssa couldn't hear me.

Francesca edged closer to me. "So what were you saying, Kaity?"

"Katya," I yelled. "My homeschool name is Katya. I was saying I don't spend a lot of time in my room. I'm actually mostly"—I needed a non-salon place to tell her—"in my tree house."

Oh, no! That sounded like I was eight! I prayed she hadn't heard me.

"Cool!" she shouted back.

So I swallowed and kept going. "Yeah, it's my workspace, actually. I've actually got it set up with everything I need." And now I was making myself sound like a hermit! "But I also get out a lot. In fact, I'm mostly out."

"That's awesome," she said. "I always thought home-schooling meant you were at home."

I nodded. "I know. But it's not true." Too late I thought, *Uh-oh! What if she asks me where I go?* I thought about telling her about the foraging, but it somehow lacked coolness, so I said, "I'm actually looking into the question of how wild plants can cure diseases."

"Oh, wow!" she said. "That sounds amazing."

"Yeah." A dancer's arm whacked me in the back. I ignored it. "I'm doing fieldwork," I said. "Field research."

"Awesome!" she said again. "You mean like those guys who go down to, like, the Amazon—"

"No. I mean, maybe. I mean, I've already made some interesting discoveries about common problems, like . . ." Dylan Davis, who was like the male version of Francesca—gorgeous, smart, and president of everything—had been hovering around. Now he moved in closer. Was he going to ask about my research? Or . . . my heart skittered . . . ask me to dance? No, it was Francesca he was eyeing, and she was flashing him her brilliant smile. But Jessie and Alyssa seemed to have given up listening to me, and were talking to him, so I kept going. ". . . like poison ivy and"—I wasn't sure if you pronounced it fun-GEE, like bungee, or fun-GUY—"funguses."

93

"Funguses. Really." Hard as it was to believe, Francesca seemed to have forgotten Dylan.

"Yes, and I'm studying the local coyote population as well as all the local plants. I love anything to do with nature." That sounded geekier than I'd hoped, so I added, "And I also met this boy."

"That mystery boy you told us about?" Jess instantly stopped flirting with Dylan. "You saw him again? Really?"

"Yep." My heart skittered again at the lie. "He's, like, this really interesting and cool violinist composer person."

"Sweet!" Francesca looked impressed. "Where'd you meet him?"

"In a field. While I was gathering edible wild plants. He was playing his violin and wearing these crazy patchwork pajamas." I couldn't tell if Jess and Alyssa's *Eew!* looks were about the plants, the pants, or the field. "I'm not always in fields, though. I go lots of other neat places. Like to"—I felt like I was stepping off a cliff, but I kept going—"New Haven. I go there at least once a week for . . . African dance classes and Zen archery." Since Rosie had never told me what that was, I added, "And I go to the Peabody Museum of Natural History a lot. With my homeschool group. Which the violinist boy belongs to too, by the way. It's called . . . the Homeschool Liberation League."

What was I doing? Wanting to make yourself look good was one thing, but I was digging myself in deeper and deeper. Except that the Peabody really *was* a brilliant idea. And if there wasn't a Homeschool Liberation League, there should be. Not to mention that Francesca had said "awesome" and "amazing" about fifty times.

"That is so awesome!" she said again. "I love it!"

So I kept on going. "Yeah, it's actually called unschooling, what I'm doing. That's where instead of being chained to a desk all day, and having it be basically just like school, except at home, you work totally independently on whatever grabs you, like . . ."—I searched for something that would grab an all-A-type person like Francesca—"my diabetes study, with this elderly man I met, and my research into the teenage brain."

With a quizzical smile, Mr. Zingarelli joined our group. "Excuse me," he said. "Did I hear somebody mention the teenage brain? At a dance?"

"Hey, Mr. Z.!" Francesca moved over to make room for him. "Kai . . . I mean, Katya's been telling us these incredibly interesting things about homeschooling. She belongs to something called the Homeschool Liberation League. Isn't that cool? And she's studying coyotes."

"So I gather," he said. "And why am I not surprised?"

I didn't dare to look at him. He knew I made things up. He'd caught my wart notes. But his voice warmed as he turned to me. "You've always been a big believer in freedom," he said. "I'm glad to hear homeschooling is working so well for you."

"Yes." Affection and gratitude flooded over me. "Yes! It is!"

I'll never know what made me look up then, but when I

did the blood drained from my head. Like an evil joke, or God punishing me for lying, there in the corner of the gym, maybe thirty feet away, standing by himself reading a book, was the boy I'd been talking about. The boy from Alvin's field. My Mystery Boy.

12

"Are you okay?" Francesca touched my arm. "Who'd you see?"

I tried hard to look normal, but I knew my face was bright red. "No one!"

"Tyler again?" Jessie's eyes scanned the room.

"No. Really. It's nobody."

Too late. The boy, no doubt feeling six sets of eyes on him, was looking our way, his hand halfway up in a should-I-be-doing-this? wave.

"Who is that?" Alyssa said, pushing Dylan aside so she could see. "Ooh, patchwork pants! Your homeschool musician boy! Kaity, did you know he was coming?"

Jessie craned to look too. "I hate the pants," she yelled. "But he's really cute. You didn't tell us he was cute. He looks old. How old is he? And why is he reading at a dance?"

"Because he's all by himself, obviously," Francesca said. "He's a homeschooler. He doesn't know anybody. You should go get him and bring him over."

"No." If my face got any redder it would catch on fire. "No! He's very shy. Painfully shy. He gets, like . . . you know . . . hives . . . when people talk to him."

"How can somebody so cute be shy?" Jessie said. "Maybe he's just allergic to you. I'll go talk to him."

"No." I blocked her path. "I'll talk to him."

The boy jumped when I tapped him on the shoulder. "Oh, man," he said, closing his book. "I was scared it was someone asking me to dance."

"No." I hoped the gum was still working. "Would you by any chance like to leave? Like right now? I need to get out of here."

His face started to relax. "Are you kidding? I've been wanting to leave from the minute I got here. Where we going?"

"I don't know. Outside. Anywhere. I'm Katya, by the way." I grabbed his hand, which I couldn't believe I was doing, having seen him exactly once before.

He looked startled, but didn't let go. "Milo," he shouted as I started heading us around the edge of the gym toward the doors. "By the way," he yelled as two sixth-grade girls almost mowed him down. "Those grapes of yours were the worst thing I ever had."

I made an apologetic face. "I know. Sorry. What are you doing here?"

"I'm with my little sister. I'm her"—he did a one-handed air quote—"'date' tonight."

I looked through the crowd, but saw no girls I didn't recognize. "Where is she?"

"Over there. With that little shrimpy dude." He pointed to a tall, thin girl in a black knit hat, black jeans, and black top, towering over a sixth-grade boy. "I told my dad that 'middle school dance' is actually a technical term for a situation in which two pieces of equipment are both waiting for the other to initiate communication, thus resulting in nothing whatsoever happening, but he still made me come with her. She's never been to a dance. She just started school this year."

We were halfway to the doors now. My hand was sweating all over him, but he made no move to pull his away.

"You don't go to school, though, right?" I asked, praying, *Please, don't make me a liar about this too.*

His eyebrow went up. "No. Unfortunately."

"Hey! Where you going?" It was Francesca, trailed by Jessie and Alyssa. "You're not leaving us?"

My heart started hammering. "Uh, yeah, sorry. Milo needs to leave."

"What? You can't leave yet." Francesca put a hand on my arm. "If you and Milo could just spare me one teensy second . . ." Those big blue eyes zoomed in on him. "Milo, I was really hoping to hear about your homeschool experience . . ."

"It bites," he said as I attempted to drag him off.

"Gotcha," she said. "Why is that?"

Jessie grabbed my hood and held me back. "I thought you said he was shy," she yell-whispered in my ear, with a meaningful glance at my hand. Which he now dropped. "Hi, Milo. I'm Jessica, and this is Al—"

Francesca cut her off. "So, then, Milo, you're saying you don't like homeschooling?"

He did that raised eyebrow thing again. "Not a lot."

Her eyes lit up. "Oh, this is so perfect! One loves it, one hates it. Wait'll I tell Mr. Z. I can make it two articles!"

"Articles?" A horrible, sick feeling started in my stomach. "You're writing an article?"

"Yeah," she said. "I'm on the paper this year. Mr. Z.'s the new advisor. He challenged me to come up with something new and different, not the usual Pep Club Gets New—"

"You mean this was an interview?" I could feel my ears getting hot even as my hands felt icy cold. "I thought you just wanted to know. I thought you were interested."

"I did. I am. It's just . . ." She was practically hopping up and down, she was so excited. "I've been going nuts trying to find something really cool to write about, and Mr. Z. said there's never been anything on homeschooling. I'm gonna call it 'Leaving School and Finding Yourself: The Case for Homeschool.' Or maybe 'From Schoolhouse to Tree House.' What do you think? I can come by next week with my photographer. We'll do, like, A Day in the Life. I can interview your mom too."

"No!" I could already see the page one photo in *The Tiger's Tale*: me in the salon, next to the whiteboard with The Dreaded DIM, surrounded by pink-rollered old ladies. "No! That won't work! I won't be home next week. At all. I'll be out."

"That's fine," Francesca said. "I'm sure Mr. Z. can get me out of school for this. I'll meet you at Zen archery. Or sit in at the Homeschool Liberation League. What do you think, Milo? Think your group will let me?"

"No!" I said as Milo stared at me blankly. "We need to leave now. Milo's promised to introduce me to his sister. She just started here. She's never been to school before. Right, Milo?"

"Right." He looked not just baffled, but like he was wishing he'd never met me. "I should go. Nice meeting all of you. See ya, Katya."

"No, don't leave me!"

As I desperately hurried after him, Francesca fell into step beside us. "So is this really, like, her first time at school, your sister? How's she liking it? If I could just tag along for a minute, and ask her a few questions? Because then this can be a three-part series, and I can definitely enter it for the Excellence in Journalism prize. But Kaity, I mean, Katya—I love that name, by the way—you're, like, this really well-known person here at school, so we totally have to start with you."

"No!" We were only about twenty feet from the doors. I was wondering what would happen if I simply ran out and ran home, when the voice I hated more than any other in the world boomed out behind me.

"Hello, Kaitlyn. This is an unexpected pleasure seeing you here."

Milo took the opportunity to leave. Making it just me, Francesca, and Mr. Westenburg.

"So Mr. Z. tells me we're running an article about you in *The Tiger's Tale*," he said with his fake-jovial, pseudo-benevolent, non-smile smile. "That must mean our little homeschooling experiment is going well."

"Oh, it is," Francesca said. "It's really exciting."

My mouth refused to open.

"So then have you sent in your official notice of withdrawal yet, Kaitlyn?" he said. "And the Notice of Intent, with your parents' proposed methods of assessment and hours of instruction? Because you know, until your parents pull you out, you're still officially a student here."

A few minutes ago I couldn't get myself to shut up. So why now, when I desperately needed to make up something to say, could I not think of a single word?

I could see three possibilities: Die; confess, and throw myself on Francesca's mercy; or come back to school Monday so there'd be no homeschool for her to write about. They all made my skin crawl. They all made me furious.

And then from somewhere in the depths of my mind came the thought: If those things I said I was doing sounded so amazing, why wasn't I doing them?

Fighting the urge to make a run for the door, I swallowed hard and prayed my voice wouldn't come out like I was being strangled. "Don't worry, Mr. Westenburg," I said. "The letter's going in tomorrow."

CHAPTER 13

CERTIFIED MAIL RETURN RECEIPT REQUESTED

To whom it may concern:

Effective September 18, I am withdrawing my child, Kaitlyn Antonucci, from the Westcott Public School District. We will comply with all requirements.

Sincerely,
Joseph C. Antonucci

I obviously couldn't tell Mom and Dad about Francesca, or the article, or the tangle of lies I'd snarled myself into. I needed a plan. I didn't have one. But it was still early enough Sunday morning that I was sure Francesca wouldn't pick up, so I left her a voice mail.

"Hey, just letting you know I'll be totally unreachable. But November twenty-ninth looks open, so if that works for you, we can do your Day in the Life thing then."

I jumped each time the phone rang that day. But it was always either Jess or Alyssa, or both together, wanting to discuss Milo, who had disappeared, never to be seen again that night, after the Westenburg encounter.

"It's better that way," I said. "Trust me."

"What are you talking about?" Jessie said. "He obviously liked you. Call him up and ask what happened."

"I can't," I said. "A, I don't like him. B, I don't have his number. Or even his last name."

"How can that be?" she said. "You're in that group together."

"I know, but . . ." My heart shrank at the thought of more lies. "It's like, you know, 'Hi, I'm Milo and I'm a home-schooler.'"

"Well, that sucks," she said. "So when do you meet again?"

"Who?"

"The group, genius."

"I don't know. They're very, kind of . . . loose."

"No prob. We'll track down his sister at school tomor-row."

"No!" I said. "Please! Just drop it, okay? Promise me you'll drop it."

I was getting Mrs. Corelli set up under the dryer the next afternoon when I got a call. It was Jessie, whispering. "Okay, her name is either Cleo or Chloe, she's wearing all black again, and she's about to get on the other bus. Should we say something to her?"

"No!" My heart jumped. "Like what?"

"Like, duh, give her your number? To give to Milo?"

"No!"

"Why not?"

"Because . . ." *I made a total fool of myself?* That would mean admitting all the stuff I'd made up. "Because I have other things to think about besides boys."

"Oh, right. Excuse me. I forgot," she said. "You have funguses. And your big interview. When's that happening?"

"Never," I said.

"That's not what Francesca said. She just told us she's coming over to see you Thursday."

"What? I said I couldn't meet with her till November!"

"Yeah, well, you know Francesca. Once she latches on to something . . ."

Heart hammering, I called Francesca again. She sounded alarmingly happy to hear from me.

"Mr. Z. is so excited about this series," she said. "And he agrees your part needs to be first. But I totally understand how busy you are, so I can just go ahead and write up what you said at the dance, if that's easier for you. Then I can stop by your house tomorrow night to run it by you, and also get your mom and dad's perspective—"

"No!" I said. "That doesn't work!"

"Gotcha," she said. "What do you suggest?"

"That you not do it!" I blurted.

"Why?"

"Because . . ." *Everything I told you is a lie?* If I couldn't tell my friends, I sure wasn't about to tell Francesca. "I'm just really kind of stressed right now."

"Oh, well . . ." She sounded disappointed. "I guess I could do it with just Milo. I was about to tell you I'm seeing him on Thursday."

"You're seeing Milo Thursday?" Mixed in with the jealousy I felt a whole new panic. "You talked to him?"

"Yes, but it wasn't easy. He's even busier than you are. Did you know he practices six hours a day? And takes two-hour violin lessons twice a week?"

"Uh . . . yeah," I lied. "But you guys didn't talk about me, did you? Or about the"—I was embarrassed even to say the name—"Homeschool Liberation League. Because no one is supposed to talk about it, even the members."

"Don't worry," she said. "I only got to talk to him for a second. Mostly I just talked to his dad about homeschooling. And he told me Milo has no lesson Thursday, so I talked Milo into meeting. I sort of implied you might be there. You don't mind, right? It was the only way I could get him to say yes."

Another wave of panic roared over me. I needed to think. I couldn't. Except that she'd just said Milo wanted to see me. And if I did meet with them, I'd have at least some chance of steering the conversation.

"Okay," I said. "But it can't be at my house. There'll be no one for you to talk to there. And nothing to see. Not even the tree house. Which, actually, my dad had to take down. It was . . . struck by lightning. It was structurally unsound."

Thank goodness she let that pass.

"No problem!" she said. "Let me just put you on hold a second! . . . Done!" she said a minute later. "We're set! Thursday at three thirty. But he doesn't want to meet at his house either. So we're meeting in some field. He said you'd know where."

wed. Sept 20
3:45 a.m.
would somebody please tell me what I'm doing??????????????

It was raining like mad when I woke up Thursday morning.

"Hey, Francesca. It's Katya. Guess our meeting's off. Call when you get this."

I left that message on her home machine and on her cell. I also texted her. She didn't answer.

Since the dance, instead of dawdling through Mom's DIM assignments, I'd been plowing through them as fast as possible to get to my own stuff. I'd already found a great medicinal plant website and set up a chart of the ones that grew around here and their uses. But with the rain letting up and then starting again, I was too edgy to work on it. Plus, we had back-to-back clients in the salon, crabby ones, who needed tea, and coffee, and a little nonfat milk for their coffee, and change for a ten, and to borrow an umbrella.

I knew Francesca couldn't call during class, but when her

lunch period came and went, all I could think was that she was waiting to see if the rain stopped completely. If it didn't, I was terrified she'd show up here. And if no one answered the door at the house, where would she go? Logic told me: upstairs, to the salon. Where she'd get to interview not only Mom, but Cookie, who'd stayed around after algebra to get her roots done.

Sure enough, I was sectioning off Cookie's hair while Mom mixed up the color when the phone rang. Almost three. Not raining. I jumped like I'd been struck by lightning.

"Could you get that, sweetie?" Mom said.

And have Francesca hear me say: "Good afternoon, A Cut Above. Katya speaking"? I let the machine get it.

"Listen, this is Eddie, Donna. I hate to cancel on you at the last minute, but with this rain and all, the arthritis is so bad I can't even reach my feet to get my shoes on. That ingrown toenail will wait till next week, I guess."

Mr. Horton! I almost fell over with relief. Even before Mom finished explaining to Cookie that something that would be nothing on someone else's foot could spell major trouble for a diabetic, I'd pulled the line of hair clips off my shirt sleeve.

"Just tell me where he lives," I said. "I'll go to his house! I'll check his feet right now! I'll take my bike."

If he lived on the other end of town, so much the better.

"You know, my cousin Lou is a diabetic," Cookie said. "They had to cut his foot off."

"You hear that, Mom?" I said. "I am definitely going."

"So you know what you're looking for on his feet, right?" she said after she'd arranged it with Mr. Horton, and explained to me where he lived, and the fastest way to get there. "You have to look at his heels, and the soles of his feet, and especially between his toes. I'm sure they're fine, but if that big toenail looks funky at all, tell him I'll be over tomorrow."

"You'll need a warm sweater under your raincoat," Cookie said. "It's freezing."

"Remember, if you see any, like, red spots or swellings or blisters, it doesn't matter how small," Mom called after me, "he has to call the doctor."

"And make sure to call if you have any questions," Cookie said. "And to let us know what happened."

What I imagined happening was that I'd get to Mr. Horton's house and find him with a horrible sore on his foot that he couldn't feel, and couldn't see. But I'd spot it. And he wouldn't want to call the doctor, but I'd talk him into it, and since he couldn't get his shoes on to drive, the ambulance would come, and the ambulance driver would tell me what a good thing I'd done. And when Francesca called to apologize for canceling, I could tell her I'd saved Mr. Horton.

That wasn't why I was doing it, though, I told myself as I went down to the house for a sweater and my poncho, and got my bike out of the garage. And this wasn't hiding from Francesca, even if it turned out that way.

Maybe on the way back I'd even find some medicinal plants that worked on diabetes.

It had started raining again when I got outside—a stinging rain that felt more like November than September. It was hard to imagine Francesca slogging through acres of wet grass onto a cold, windy field, even to get her story. But Milo might. Francesca said he wanted to see me. I remembered the way his hand had felt in mine—like it wanted to be held. Mr. Horton lived at the end of Hunter Brook Road. If I took the back way, I could ride by Alvin's field and check if anyone was there.

The road was slick with leaves and the wind was so strong, my poncho billowed out behind me like a sail. I hunched low over the handlebars, worrying that a car would pull up alongside me and that it would be Francesca's mother. But there was no one on the road at all. And when I passed the field, it was, of course, deserted.

I'd already turned onto Hunter Brook Road when the thought hit me: What if Francesca showed up while I was gone and interviewed Mom? I could hear Cookie already: "Oh yes, Kaity's a wonderful assistant. And a quick study. Her mother would be lost without her." And Mom: "Unschooling? No, no, we don't believe in unschooling."

But as I rode across the little concrete bridge I saw something that made me forget Francesca. At first, all I saw was the big downed tree, with a stump that looked like it had gone through a pencil sharpener. Then I noticed that the wood chips were so fresh they weren't even wet. I'd seen beaver dams and lodges all around here, but never a beaver. How cool would that be, I thought, to actually see a beaver drag a tree away. I stopped my bike and leaned it up against the bridge and looked over. Hunter Brook, usually a peaceful little stream, was all churned up and foamy, and over its banks. Which, I now noticed, had no trees on either side, just pointy stumps. This was like, beaver heaven. No beaver, though, unfortunately. Or . . . wait . . . what was that furry object lying under the tree trunk? Was my imagination going wild again, or was it a squashed beaver?

14

"Door's open," Mr. Horton shouted when I rang the bell.

I heard the click of toenails. Then a barrel-shaped husky with one blue eye and one brown shambled out to greet me.

"Did you ever hear of a beaver getting killed by a tree?" I called as I added my sneakers to the heap of boots and shoes by the mudroom door. "Because there's a dead beaver, right down the road!" I followed the dog through a yellow kitchen, with a revolving tray full of pill bottles on the table, into the living room, where Mr. Horton, looking like he hadn't washed his face or combed his hair in a while, sat with his legs up in an overstuffed recliner. "In the marsh right past the bridge!" I told him. "He got pinned by a tree!"

Mr. Horton put his magazine down. "And you know he was dead? Did you check?"

"No," I said. "But it was a gigantic tree." I remembered the dry wood chips all around it. "But you're right! It could've just fallen. I'll ride back and see."

"No." He hoisted himself to his feet. "We'll take the truck. That way if he is still alive, we can winch the tree off him. You may need to give me a hand with my boots, though. I'm not sure I can bend over far enough to lace 'em up."

With a promise to check his feet when we got back, I laced the boots and helped him zip his rain jacket. He walked out to the truck okay. But once we'd parked by the bridge, and I got a good look at the rough, brushy ground between us and the tree, I wondered if his legs were too stiff to make it down the bank.

"Can you see him yet?" he called after me as I bashed through the wet brambles, then climbed over the masses of leaves and branches and broken sticks to get to the fallen tree. "How's he look? Is he moving at all? Can you tell if he's breathing?"

"Not yet." I hated the dorky visor thing on my poncho, but it was pouring so hard I was glad to have it. After checking that I wasn't about to be jumped by the beaver's grief-crazed brother, I stepped closer, cursing as my sneaker sank into the mud. "No, he's not moving!" The trunk had to be twelve inches around. It had to weigh a ton. A beaver caught under it wouldn't stand a chance. But as I slogged my way through the mud to the other side of the tree, I could see that he wasn't squashed flat. Only the back end and part of the tail were pinned. I'd always thought a beaver was woodchuck-sized. This beaver was bigger than Waffle, thick and solidly muscled. I couldn't tell if his nose was buried in the mud, or if his eyes were open. But the wet brown fur was sleek and unmarked.

"I don't see any blood," I called. I kneeled on the log and

carefully, my heart pounding, peered down at him. Then I dug my cell phone from my pocket, leaned closer, and got a picture. He tensed, and one foot did a scrabbling thing. "Mr. Horton!" I shouted. "He's alive! He knows I'm looking at him!"

"Hold on!" he yelled back. "I'm coming down. But I'm gonna need a hand with this."

I hurried back to the pickup. From behind the seat, Mr. Horton pulled two lengths of chain, a pair of work gloves, and a red metal jack-like thing with a heavy hook on each end.

"First thing to do is find a tree close to the fallen one," he said as he started down the bank, not totally hobbling, but stiff enough to make me nervous.

"Here, wait." I picked up a sturdy-looking stick and brought it to him. "And let me take that chain."

"Thanks," he said, using the stick to steady himself as he carefully picked his way down. "So we're gonna wrap one chain around the standing tree, the other around the log, attach a hook on both and—"

I was way ahead of him. "How's that one?" I pointed to a young maple. "Think it's big enough?"

He pushed back his hunting cap and wiped his face. "It don't need to be big. But you're gonna want it to be a lot closer to the base of the log, so we're not lifting the whole tree. And you're gonna need to find us enough space under the log to pass the other chain through, close as you can get to the beaver. Just don't let him bite you."

I gulped. "Beavers bite?"

"It's a wild animal," he said. "You'd bite too, if you were trapped under a log."

I kneeled in the mud and crawled along looking for a place where a bump or branch held the trunk off the ground. Crawling while carrying a chain was not fun. The poncho's flapping sides kept snagging on broken branch ends, or getting caught under my knees. The cold, clay-like mud soaked through my jeans and packed in under my fingernails. The tree seemed to have totally sunk into it.

"I don't see anyplace," I said, sitting up to wipe my nose.

Mr. Horton had already picked out a maple tree across from the beaver and wrapped the chain around it several times, above a heavy branch. "How 'bout there?" He pointed to a spot only a few feet from the beaver. He bent over and craned his neck. "Yeah, I think can I see a little daylight under there!"

I gulped again and crawled closer. "Okay." Keeping a cautious eye on the beaver, I unwrapped the chain from my arm and tried pushing it through the space. It barely fit, so I found a stick and scratched out a trough under the tree and shoved the chain in. No reaction from the beaver. Which was both good and bad. I jumped up, climbed over the log, and using my stick like a crochet hook, wiggled the chain through.

"Now we're in business!" said Mr. Horton. We tugged through enough chain to encircle the trunk. Then he attached the ends together with one of the two hooks. "Now you're gonna see why this thing is called a come-along," he said. "It's got a cog with a catch, so it can't slip. And now"—he pulled out the come-along's cable to its full length—"we attach the other hook to our maple, and then, if my hands still work well enough to crank this baby, we'll be copasetic!" He hooked up the other end of the cable. "Okay now. Move well away," he warned as he pushed down on the come-along's lever. "Once this tree starts to move, you don't want to be anywhere nearby."

I jumped up and stepped back into the brush.

He pushed again, and then again. The cable tightened. His face was getting red.

"Is it hard?" I asked, not sure whether to offer to help, stay here and watch, or go back and see how the beaver was doing.

"Only when you've got this damn arthritis." He pumped again. "But then, I wasn't sure my legs would get me down the hill, and they did." He gave another pump. "So we'll just hope the hands will . . . Here we go!"

The cable was taut now. I could see the hook straining. And then the trunk began to move—a fraction of an inch, then another fraction.

"Will it hold?" I asked. "Is it gonna break? It's not gonna break, right, because if it does that beaver's toast."

"Pancake's more like it. But don't worry." He pumped again. "This baby's lifted bigger logs than this. How's the beaver doing?"

"Not moving. No, wait, his foot just moved again! It's like he's trying to get away."

"Well, tell him to hold on. We're almost there."

With a creak, the trunk rose another little bit.

"How high do we need to get it?" I asked.

"Just high enough to let off the pressure—"

Before I could blink, the beaver had slid out from under, and with a loud snuff, scuttled for the stream, where he plopped in, slapped the water with his tail, and disappeared.

"Hey! You're welcome!" Mr. Horton yelled after him. "That's gratitude for you!" He turned to me. "Well, at least you didn't have to give him CPR—"

"Mr. Horton!" I cut him off as a thought hit me. "You think the same thing that lets beavers breathe underwater is what kept him from suffocating in the mud?"

"Dunno," he said. "But I'll see if we can find something in one of my magazines when we get back. Oh, man!" He shook his head. "The boys down at the Dutch Treat are never gonna believe this." He chuckled. "CPR to a beaver . . . I can just hear you! 'You're a great guy, Bucky, but next time brush your teeth before you—'"

"What makes you think he's a guy?" I cut him off again. "He could have been Buckerina. With a lodge full of little beavers. We could have just saved the whole Hunter Brook beaver population. And I could have just made my first scientific discovery!"

15

"So, you know that TV show called *Dirty Jobs*?" Mr. Horton ran a hand through his hair, which was still sticking out like gray feathers. "Where the guy goes around to pig farms and sewage disposal plants, and they're always saying, 'It's nasty work, but someone's gotta do it'?"

We were back in his kitchen, washed up and relatively dry. It had taken forever to pull the chains off and out from under the log, two trips to get the gear to the truck, and another long time to help Mr. Horton up the muddy slope.

I helped myself to a few chips from the bag he'd put out and took a sip of tea. "Are we still talking about CPR on the beaver?" He'd chuckled about that the whole ride back to his house.

"No. My feet." He looked embarrassed suddenly. "Unless you need to get home."

"No, no."

With his dog Buddy sniffing my face, I sat cross-legged on the floor in front of Mr. Horton. He didn't say anything as I peeled the first sock over his knobby ankle bone, but as I got to the second sock, he began to look awkward again.

"They're not stinking you out, are they?" he asked. "I had a little trouble getting 'em off last night."

"They smell better than my dad's," I said.

He laughed. "That's a ringing endorsement. How do they look?"

Not as bad as his legs, I thought. I'd never seen ankles as lumpy, or so many thready blue and purple veins. I didn't feel grossed out, though, for some reason. Carefully as I could, remembering everything Mom had said, I examined the tops and bottoms of each foot, and the heels, and checked between his toes. Which were also knobby and gross. But I didn't see anything that looked not right. The big toenail didn't seem ingrown.

"I think they're okay," I said.

"Well then," he said. "Just get me a pair of clean socks from the dryer over there and we'll call this dirty job done."

I eyed the tray of pill bottles as I pulled the new socks on for him. "So, if you don't mind my asking, are arthritis and diabetes two different things? Or do they go together?"

"I don't mind your asking," he said. "I just mind having them. Diabetes is a disease where your blood sugar is too high. The sugar can't get into your cells, so it stays in your blood. Arthritis makes your joints swell and hurt."

"And do people . . ." I made a face so I wouldn't have to say it.

"Die of them? Not from the arthritis. Arthritis just makes you feel like you're a hundred years old and can't do what you want to do, and pisses you off beyond belief. But the diabetes can lead to a whole bunch of nasty things." He sighed. "But I monitor my blood sugar, and take my insulin injections, and try to eat right, mostly anyway, and do what I can to take care of myself. Which is why I go see your mom every week. That, and because it's kind of nice having someone to fuss over me again."

"She's a fusser, all right," I said because he was starting to look sad, and this was making me upset. I both wanted to know more and didn't. I stood up. "I should go." It was almost five thirty. I couldn't believe Mom hadn't called. Though that was great news. It meant no Francesca. Who hadn't called me either, now that I thought of it. I checked my cell in case I'd missed any calls down at the swamp. Nothing. *Whew.*

As if on cue, his phone rang.

"She's just leaving, Donna," he said. "Yup, the feet are fine. We're just having some tea and shooting the breeze and then I'm going to find her some reading material. I thought I'd leave you to tell her about our little adventure," he added to me when he hung up. "Now let's find you them articles."

I'd been too worried about the beaver to notice the living room before. It was a strange mix of lace curtains, fusty old plants, and china figurines, like my aunt Angie's living room, and antlers. Not only over the fireplace. The narrow shelf up by the ceiling was total antlers.

"You've got a lot of antlers here," I said as he searched through the stacks of magazines cramming the bookcase: *National Geographic, Wildlife Conservation, Field & Stream.*

He pulled out a couple for me. "I've got a lot of all kinds of crap." He showed me a snapping turtle shell as big as our turkey platter under the coffee table. And piles of papery, shriveled snake skins, a few with rattles. Drawers of birds' nests of all sizes, all labeled. Shoe boxes of bones, also labeled. A branch with a wasp nest the size of a beach ball. A tray of arrowheads. Even a lumpy, mangy-looking stuffed squirrel.

"It's not crap at all!" I said. "It's a nature museum."

"That's not what my wife called it!" He dug around in the coat closet till he found a plastic bag for the magazines. "I used to have to keep it all down cellar. I worked for the phone company, you know, so I was out driving the back roads all day long, and on my breaks I'd poke around in the woods and see what I could see. And if that sometimes meant I spent a little more time out and about than some people would've liked, well . . ." He shrugged and smiled.

I nodded. "Sounds like me!"

His smile faded. "I can't do that anymore, I'm sad to say."

I made a face. "Me neither."

"But I still take the truck out for a look around most mornings, just park and watch the sun come up and see what walks by."

"Like what?" I said.

"Well, my best sighting was two bobcats playing in the snow. But a couple weeks ago, I saw a family of coyotes, two big ones and two pups, just as the sun was coming up. Right out past you, in fact."

"Out past me where? A couple of weeks ago? Seriously, four at one time?" In my excitement I knocked over a coffee can of turkey feathers. "What'd they look like? How big were they?"

"Kinda like German shepherds, only blonder, and with puffier tails, and they hold their tails different." He waved a hand at me to leave the feathers and smiled. "Them pups were cuter'n hell. You know, there might still be a chance to see them. The family groups start breaking up in autumn, but if we get out there right at sunup—"

"We?" I said. "Like you and me?"

"Why not?" he said. "If we miss the coyotes, we can always pull up some spotted knapweed and garlic mustard. And you can help me chop some Asiatic bittersweet. I try to do that every time I go out. You know, do my little bit to slow the alien invasion." He must have seen I had no clue what he was talking about, because he rummaged in a drawer, then handed me a folded-up poster: Invasive Plants of Connecticut. "It's the plant version of a Ten Most Wanted list. Keep it if you want. I already know all the alien invaders."

I still didn't know what he was talking about. I didn't care. I loved Mr. Horton.

There was no sign of Bucky/Buckerina as I rode by on my way home. But I decided to set the alarm for an hour early tomorrow morning and shoot over for another look. I couldn't wait to get home and Google beaver squashings and tell Dimitri. Maybe I'd tell Rosie too. And maybe after the salon tomorrow, I'd go over and tell Mrs. Williams.

I was so pumped I was almost home before I remembered Francesca.

"So did anything happen after I left?" I asked Mom. She and Dad were in the kitchen, per usual, making dinner. "No one showed up unexpectedly, right? Did anybody call?"

She glanced up from chopping garlic. "For you, you mean?"

"Yeah, you don't say hi anymore?" Dad was slicing sausage. "Or why your pants are covered with mud? I thought you were making a house call to Mr. Horton. How'd that go? Mom said you did good."

"I did," I said. "And they're almost dry now. Did anybody call?"

"Well," Mom said. "You got an interesting call from Francesca Halloran."

Even though I'd been expecting it, a jolt went through me. "She called the salon?"

"Yes." She scraped her knife off on the board. "That's great you guys are friends again."

"We're not." I went over to the counter. "Mom, what'd she say?"

"Something about how she was supposed to be meeting you and she was afraid you were up on Alvin's field waiting for her. I told her no, you were out making a home visit, taking care of a client."

"Client?" My heart jolted again. "You didn't say anything about the salon, did you? What'd she say to that?"

"She said, 'Oh, wow.' Then she started going on about some article she's doing for the school paper, something about a day in the life, and how she'd really love to get the mom's-eye view of homeschooling, and what is my philosophy of homeschooling and my views on unschooling."

I braced myself. "And what'd you say?"

Mom had this look she gets when she's trying to milk a story for all it's worth. I held my breath.

"I said, 'Francesca, what are those noises I keep hearing?' Because I could hear all these beeps and commotion, and carts clanking in the background. And you know what she said?" Mom turned to Dad. "Do you believe this, Joe? She said, 'I'm in the emergency room. I think I may need an operation.'"

Dad looked up from his slicing. "She's calling from the emergency room to ask your philosophy of homeschooling?"

"Yeah, and get this," Mom said. "Then she goes, 'And I'm so upset! They're saying my appendix is about to burst and I haven't finished my article!'"

I felt like the beaver must have when the log was lifted.

I threw my arms around Mom. "Oh, *whew*! Thank goodness! That's the best news! Not the appendix, the article! Mom, you just saved my life! Speaking of which, Dad, did you ever hear of a come-along?" I pulled out my cell to show them the picture. "Mr. Horton and I used one to rescue a beaver!"

CHAPTER 16

Appendix operations, from everything I read online, were totally routine. Francesca would be out of the hospital in a day, back to school in a few weeks. In fact, she'd probably be on the phone to me as soon as the anesthesia wore off. But for the moment, I was free!

I was up till two that night, reading about beavers and invasive plants, and finding great stuff on the Internet about all sorts of things.

⊠ To: Ask the Science Man
Subject: Re: "DO THE TREES BEAVERS CUT DOWN
EVER FALL ON AND SQUISH THE BEAVERS?"
You told "Curious in Maine" that there are only two squished beaver reports in the science literature, one from 1953, and one in 1989.

Well, make that three! Here is the (somewhat blurry—it was raining) picture I took on my cell today to prove it. But this beaver was not mortally squished, I'm happy to say. My friend and I freed him. Unfortunately he ran away before I could take another picture.

I need to report this to the right people so that the literature can be updated. I got the name of the journal with the 1953 article and wrote to them. Please tell me what else I should do.

I also just read that beavers' ears and noses have a valve that closes to keep the water out when they're submerged. My theory is that this is how this one survived having his face pressed in the mud. What do you think? Please answer as soon as possible so I can report this too.

I sent the link and my beaver pic to Dimitri and Rosie too—my first e-mail to her in two weeks, although she hadn't written to me either.

✉ hey rosie, sorry i disappeared on u. things here kinda sucked for a while. some of it still does (mom = teacher ☹) but i LOVE homeschooling again, u will b happy 2 know.

It was harder than ever now being cooped up in the salon the next day. It poured again, so didn't get over to the swamp. All day I braced myself for Francesca's call. Till I realized that maybe, after an almost-burst appendix, I wasn't number one on Francesca's mind. But I didn't hear from Science Man, or Dimitri or Rosie, or Mr. Horton either.

"I'm afraid our little adventure did me in," he said when I called to see if he wanted to go look for coyotes the next morning or chop down invasive aliens. "The spirit's willing. But the joints ain't able."

Who wanted to come out with me the next morning was Dad. Not on a coyote hunt. He pointed out, reasonably enough, that we weren't too likely to see coyotes at nine in the morning. But since it was one of the rare Saturdays he didn't have to work, he said pulling weeds sounded like a great idea.

"They're not just weeds, Dad," I said as we got gloves and tools from the garage. "It's like a plant horror movie, this whole alien invasives thing. Except instead of a mad scientist, you've got some gardener who spots some plant in, in this case, Asia, and decides it'd look great climbing on his garden wall. So he brings it to this country and plants it, and the bittersweet goes, 'Oh, yeah, I love it here.' And then birds eat the berries, and poop the seeds out everywhere they fly, and the seeds sprout, and next thing we know, this alien species is spreading through our woods, growing sixty-foot-long vines, winding itself around the trees until it strangles them. Same thing with barberry and honeysuckle, which were brought over from Japan. And garlic mustard only got to our area a few years ago, but it's moving in everywhere. Do you know garlic mustard, Dad?"

He'd been organizing the garden tools while I talked. He stopped now and gave me an amused look. "You mean the stuff I've been begging you to help me weed all summer? All along the stone wall and around the compost bins, where I can't mow? Oh yeah, I know garlic mustard."

"But did you know it releases a chemical that stops other plants' seeds, including trees, from sprouting? And that the chemical kills off the good plants? And that deer won't eat it, because it tastes like mustard and garlic, which is of course why the colonists brought it to this country in the first place, to eat as greens—"

He reached across the workbench and rubbed my head. "You're preaching to the choir, honey!" He handed me a trowel and a weeding knife. "Let's weed some garlic mustard!"

The sun was hot today, but the ground was still so wet that in only a few minutes we'd pulled out the twenty or so garlic mustard plants growing around the compost bins— some young and small, but others two feet tall, and all smelling like rancid garlic. We moved on to the stone wall in front of the house, where, as he'd said, there were a gazillion more. We needed the knives here; most of the roots were growing under or between the stones.

Dad kneeled in front of a giant clump. "I've been saying it feels like this stuff's taking over the world," he said. "Now I know why."

"And wait'll you hear about spotted knapweed," I told him as, sitting cross-legged next to him, I dug the dirt out from around a big, nasty root. "Each knapweed produces thousands of seeds, and each seed can live in the soil for like, years, and the plants use up the nutrients in the soil so other plants can't grow." I pried out the root and chucked the garlic mustard plant over the wall. "It's already infested millions of acres of grazing land across the entire country!"

"That's not good," Dad said. "Oh, man, check out the roots on this bad boy!" He held up the humongous garlic mustard he'd just pulled.

"Good one!" I said, starting on one even bigger. "You know, I should go tell Adele Williams to cut down her barberry bushes. Or we could do it for her." I twisted my knife under the base. It didn't budge. "I mean, if birds really are spreading barberries all over the planet—"

"So why do people keep planting them?" he said. "Why do garden centers even sell them?"

"Exactly! Good question!"

The roots on this one seemed to go all the way to China. Dad began prying out rocks so I could get at it.

"Whoa, take a look at this guy!" With a mischievous grin, he dangled a giant earthworm. "A few more of these and we'll need to go fishing!"

"Eeew! Dad!" I flinched.

He laughed. "I thought you're supposed to like worms if you love nature. You can't have a good garden without worms. Worms are—"

"Speaking of worms," I said so he wouldn't go off on his whole wonders-of-compost routine. "Did you know that the real name for your appendix is vermiform appendix, because it's shaped like a worm? *Verm* being 'worm' in Latin. And that its biological purpose is a mystery?"

"Nope," he said. "Can't say I did."

I felt a rush of pride. "Yeah, it just kind of sits there, attached to your large intestine, not bothering anyone, unless it gets infected. By the way, Dad, did you know Norwegian has a word for dunking someone's face in the snow? *Kryne.* I read that last night. And *sludd* means wet snow. I love that! And did you know the Albanians have twenty-seven different words for mustache?"

"Really?" He had this funny, slightly puzzled almost-smile—sort of benevolent, but also like if Mom were here, he'd be catching her eye, possibly rolling his.

"Am I talking too much?" I said. "Should I, like, shut up and dig?"

"What?" He looked up. "No. No. I guess I was just thinking how long it's been since we hung out, just you and me." He levered out another rock, exposing the mother of all roots. "You can get under that with your knife now. Or I—"

"I'll do it!" I scrabbled out the soil around the root, spraying dirt on both of us. Then I got to my knees, yanked out the entire plant, and, with a "So long, sucker!" tossed it across the wall.

Who'd have guessed it could be so much fun digging weeds with your dad?

"This is fun," I said, looking over the clump of garlic mustard for the biggest one. "I could do stuff like this all day long."

"I know what you mean." There was that funny smile again. "Now, what were you saying about Norwegian mustaches?"

"Nothing important." *Did* he know what I meant? "I just thought it was cool."

"It is cool," he said. "I'm learning all sorts of things from you I didn't know."

"And I can tell you lots more too." I dug out a potato-shaped rock and wondered if I should try really talking to him. Except for my foraged feast, and blurting out about the beaver, I'd told them nothing. My mind jumped to those pitiful, middle-of-the-night letters I wrote. Could it be that my Dear . . . who????? was Dad? "I'm actually working on a few projects," I started. "Real science, Dad, not some lame module Mom's found somewhere on the Internet. But I won't get anywhere with them if I'm stuck in the salon with her all . . ."

Even without looking I could feel him stiffen.

"Oh, Kaity," he said. "You're not starting this again, are you? I thought we were just out having a nice time."

"No, we are," I said. "We are. I just thought maybe you could get her to drop the stupid DIM and ease up." I should never have said "stupid." Everything in me told me to back off. But I'd held it in for so long. And that "starting this again" really rubbed me the wrong way. "I'm suffocating in there! Dad," I said. "I need to get out!"

"Mom's doing everything she can to make it work for both of you," he said. "You know that."

I hated the way his voice sounded.

"I know I know that!"

"Well, you don't seem to get it."

"And you don't seem to get that it's as stupefying as school!" The root I was hacking at refused to come loose.

131

"I don't want to know how to do the bookkeeping or flush out the foot spa!"

"Oh, and you really think Mom does?"

"No, but it's the life she chose," I said. "I didn't—"

"That's right. So she could be her own boss, instead of working for somebody else. So she could do things her own way. Sound familiar?"

"Why are you making this about Mom?" I chopped at the root and didn't look at him. "She managed perfectly well in the salon before me."

"That has nothing to do with this. We are not dropping the DIM. And you can't just be 'out.' We've got no one to measure your progress except your mom. And the only way to measure it is to set goals. You've got high school coming up next year, and then college, and if you stick with the science—"

"What do you mean, 'stick with the science'? Science is my goal. I'm doing science."

"Yeah, that's why you're gonna need the credentials, and that doesn't mean some lousy GED diploma, like your brothers."

"Who said anything about a GED diploma?"

We were both jabbing away at the ground pretty ferociously now.

Then, out of the corner of my eye, I saw him shake his head.

"What?" I demanded.

His mouth was curled in an ironic smile.

"What's so funny?"

"Just that we're not fighting over you wanting to go out with some *jabone,* or get your butt tattooed. We're sitting here in the dirt fighting over you wanting to study science! I should be thanking God you want to be studying anything, right? I mean, how often do you hear of that happening these days?"

"Exactly!" My anger slid away. I could feel hope rising again. "And you're right. I am like her. We both need to do things our own way. I mean, that thing I learned about beavers' breathing valves? How many people know that? And it wasn't just in some textbook where I'd read it and forget it. I saw it with my own eyes, Dad. That's real biology. And this is real botany. And you wouldn't believe all the great stuff Mr. Horton's got. I can work at his house. I don't need all this social studies, and geog . . ." This time I stopped myself even before his hand went up. "I know. Shut up, Katya!"

"You don't have to shut up," he said. "You're telling me you've got dreams. I'm all for dreams, kiddo. It's how we get from here to there that we're working on, okay?"

He gave me a long zoomed-in, bunched-eyebrow, but not totally un-understanding look.

I nodded. "Okay," I said.

"Now . . ." He looked up at the sun and checked his watch. "Do we keep weeding, or say we've done our bit for the planet and go get ourselves another breakfast? How's a bacon and egg sandwich sound to you? We don't have to tell your mother."

We hadn't done that since grade school.

"Okay," I said again.

The tables at the Dutch Treat were filled when we got there, so we walked over to the counter, stopping for Dad to say hi to people, and tell them how he had no business having two breakfasts, and introduce me as his "brainy daughter." He seemed to know everyone, except for the two guys at the far end of the counter: a tight-faced man with one of those ye olde beard-but-no-mustache things, and—my heart gave a jump—was that kid in the white dress shirt and black pants and slicked-down hair, hunched over a plate of pancakes, Milo? And that girl in black had to be his sister.

"Milo!" Even before he looked up, I could feel my face explode into a smile. I lifted my hand to wave, ready to go over.

His eyes met mine for an instant. Then he went back to his pancakes.

His dad was staring at me. "Who is that girl?" I heard him ask Milo. "I don't think I know her."

"No one, Dad." Milo practically spit the words out. "It's nobody. Stop looking."

Dad would have told me if I had dirt on my face. So was it that I had on Sean's puke green plaid flannel? Or had Francesca blabbed to him about the Homeschool Liberation League? Or told him that ridiculous thing I said about the hives? Were there more things I'd made up that I didn't even remember now?

Our egg sandwiches took forever to come. Dad dawdled over his, stopping between bites to tell me how good it was, asking for two refills on his coffee, then debating having a piece of apple pie. I needed the bathroom, but no way was I walking past Milo.

I had to go too badly, though. When Dad finally got up to pay, I hurried, head down, past the counter to the restroom. When I came out of the stall, Milo's sister was standing by the sink. She looked embarrassed.

"Milo said to give you this," she said, handing me a folded-up napkin.

I waited for her to leave before I read it.

Katya, will you be anywhere near the field later? If so, I'll be there late afternoon.

CHAPTER 17

The second I got home I called Jessie, then Alyssa, to discuss what time "late afternoon" might be, and why he'd write "if so" when he had no way of finding out my answer, and what to wear. We decided on four forty-five, no makeup, hair down, and my apple green J. Crew V-neck, which they agreed brought out the green speckle-y things in my eyes and looked good enough to cancel out the puke-colored flannel.

I managed somehow to stay at home till four, then forced myself to walk slowly and notice things along the way, like the toxic-looking yellow mushrooms that had sprung up after the rain, and the Virginia creeper vines, which had turned a glowing burgundy. But my brain still raced with questions, like what I was going to do when he brought up Francesca? And how to explain the stupid Homeschool Liberation League.

Luckily, I'd stuck the weeding knife and clippers in my backpack. So, when I got to the top of the field and he wasn't there, I didn't stand around worrying. I scouted the brushy edge of the woods for barberry bushes.

I'd clipped off almost an entire three-foot bush when Milo, still in the black-and-white clothes and looking really tense, walked up, stopped a little ways away, and eyed the tangle of cut branches. "What're you doing?" he said. His hair was still all slicked down and neat, which made him look weirdly young. And strangely handsome.

Not cute, though. Jessie was wrong. His eyes were too deep-set, his eyebrows way too strong, his mouth a little too ironic. Not to mention the strange haircut, which even hair gel couldn't hide. But then no one, except possibly Cookie, called me cute either. I sat back on my heels and bit at a thorn in my thumb. "Eradicating an invasive species," I said. "But I forgot to bring gloves."

I could see him noting my scratched arms. "And you're doing this why?"

"To keep them from taking over the world," I said.

He kicked the branches into less of a barricade around me and more of a pile. One snagged on his pants leg. He pulled it free, then took a step closer. "You mean like the Norway rat and the sea squirt?"

I looked at him. "Excuse me?"

"Sea squirts? Those gross spongy little guys that make giant colonies on the ocean floor, and on, like, rocks and docks, and crowd out all the native, good stuff?" He raised an eyebrow at me. "You don't know about them?"

"Uh-uh."

"How about zebra mussels and fire ants?" He stepped closer still.

137

He was standing almost right over me now. I was glad I hadn't listened to Alyssa, who'd thought I should wear that vanilla body mist Tyler loved. Milo was so not Tyler. "So you're interested in this stuff too?" I was beginning to relax a little. If he was thinking about sea squirts, he wasn't thinking about Francesca.

"Nah," he said. "It's just, they don't let us watch regular TV at home. Only PBS. So I know all sorts of useless stuff. Like that incredibly pompous thing I said to you at the dance? About 'middle school dance' being a technical term?" He kicked another branch out of the way. "Why would I say that?"

"Because it's interesting?" I said. "Like that Albanian has twenty-seven words for mustache. You're gonna mess up your shoes. Those thorns are sharp."

He stuck his shiny black dress shoe under a whole pile of branches and flipped it aside. "I had a performance this afternoon," he said. "That's where I was till now."

"Really?" I sat back and hugged my arms around my knees. "You mean, like, a solo?"

"At my teacher's," he said. "It was no big thing. I just played a couple pieces."

"How'd it go?" I said.

He made a face. "Not great. My dad was pretty pissed, actually."

I nodded. "He looked kind of tense at the restaurant."

"And that was before the concert. You should have seen him after."

138

My heart sped up a little, but I said it anyway: "I was wondering why you were acting like you didn't know me."

"That was kind of rude, wasn't it? But I didn't want to get into it with him, you know what I'm saying?" He kicked at another branch. "I'm a little surprised you are even here this afternoon."

"Yeah, well . . ." I held up my clippers. "I had this whole field full of invasive aliens to eradicate, you know."

"Right." His face unknotted into a smile, the first I'd seen from him today. "So which evil weeds are we looking for?"

"Really? You want to help?" I pulled the Invasive Plants of Connecticut poster from my backpack and unrolled it onto a bare patch of ground for him to see. He squatted next to me. As he reached out to keep it from rolling up again, our hands brushed. A zing of electricity ran through me. "I don't think we want to do more barberries without gloves," I said. "But there's spotted knapweed." I pointed to a purple flower over by the milkweed, then showed it to him on the poster. "It's totally evil. And I'm sure there's garlic mustard. Garlic mustard is everywhere."

He jumped to his feet. "Then let's go eradicate it."

"So do you live near here?" I asked as we set off across the top of the field. It was windy, but so gorgeous, with the rippling grasses, and those puffy cotton candy clouds, and the birches on the hills behind us shining yellow in the sun. I felt almost giddy with happiness.

"Pretty near," he said.

I reached down for a stalk of grass to chew. It was tough and stringy, but it tasted delicious. "Then how come I've never seen you anywhere?"

"Possibly because I never go anywhere except lessons and rehearsals and homeschool group events?" he said, pulling a stalk for himself. It was so long it bobbled as he talked. "But it's not true you don't see me. You've seen me three times in the last two weeks."

"Uh . . ." Did I dare tell him? "Four, actually." I explained about hearing him playing his violin on the field that first night. "You almost scared me to death!" I did not add that I'd pictured him as a crazed hermit.

Even so, his eyebrow went up. "Great," he said. "All my worst moments."

"Yeah, well . . ." I made a face. "You've seen mine."

"How so?"

"If you don't know, you think I'm gonna tell you?" Subject change time! "So you should be in high school now, right?" I asked. "How old are you?"

"Fifteen," he said. "And you?"

I'd chewed all the good part of my grass stalk. I picked another. Thirteen sounded so lame. Even fourteen seemed marginal.

But when I told him the truth, I felt another rush of gladness, because he said, "Yeah, well, I'm actually not totally fifteen yet. My birthday's in November."

"So then if you went to school, you'd be in, like, tenth grade, or ninth?"

He shrugged. "One of the two. But I don't see it happening."

"Why not? They let your sister go."

"Because she's a regular person, not a musician. Which means my mom gets to have a say in the matter."

I had to learn to raise my eyebrow like that!

"My mom has too much say in the matter," I said.

"What matter is that?"

"What I do with my life," I said, which made me think of the talk with Dad this morning. "So if you don't go to high school, how does it work for, like, getting into college? I mean, can you? And do you have to take all the tests, like the PSATs and SATs? Or is it, like, not an issue, because you already know you're gonna be a musician, because I know you practice, like, six hours a day—"

His eyes narrowed. "Who told you that? Francesca?"

"No," I said. "I mean, yes, but . . ."

Subject change time again! Except that all roads seemed to lead to Francesca. I shut up and kept walking.

"You realize we're not eradicating any weeds," he said as we reached the boggy part at the edge of the woods.

"You're right," I said.

"Have you been looking?" he said.

"Not really." I made a sheepish face. "Have you?"

"Nope," he said. "I was just trying to keep up with you."

Fortunately, I spotted a group of vine-smothered trees on the other side of the stone wall. The vines had orange berries. "Well, there's some bittersweet," I said. "Which is truly evil. Too bad I don't have another pair of clippers."

"My knife's got a saw blade," he said. "Of course, it's the size of a nail file—"

"Hey, these wrists rescued a rodent," I said remembering how my six *F*s in one sentence had gotten a smile from him that first time we met.

It worked this time too. "Then my blade can totally beat a bittersweet," he said. "What rodent?"

I told him about Bucky/Buckerina. The bittersweet vines, though, were thick and woody, and so twisted together, it'd be hard to get a grip on them with the clippers, never mind saw through them with the puny Swiss Army blade. You could barely see the tree trunks under the vines, or tell what kind of trees they were.

He squatted beside the biggest one. "You're right. This stuff is as bad as kudzu."

"Kudzu?" I sat down next to him.

"Another evil alien invader," he said. "You need to start watching PBS." He didn't remember where kudzu came from, but he said the vines could grow a foot a day, and that a farmer on the show said you had to keep close watch on your cows or the kudzu would grow right over them. "And you have to close your windows at night," he added, sawing away. "Or it'll grow right over you."

"They should call it kudzilla," I said. Which was dumb, but got a laugh from him.

The vine I'd started on was so thick, I couldn't squeeze the clippers closed.

"Let me try," he said, handing me the saw instead. Which worked better for me. While I sawed, I told him the same how-bittersweet-arrived-in-this-country story I'd told Dad. It hit me that I was having basically the same comfortable time with Milo I'd had—pre-fight—with Dad this morning. Except for the constant, buzzy awareness that if I reached out my hand, or stretched my leg, I'd be touching him. Had he had girlfriends? I wondered. This felt so different from any boy/girl thing I'd ever had before. Did he have one now?

"So aside from music," I said, "do you have, like—"

"A life?" He made a face. "Depends how you define it."

"I was gonna say . . ." I felt awkward suddenly. "I mean, you must know a lot of like, cool musicians and interesting homeschoolers."

Arrgh. I sounded like Francesca!

"Well, I don't know how cool and interesting they are," he said. "They're pretty much the same kids I've known since I was three. Except for one." His mouth twisted.

I nodded. "Me too. I mean, you met my friends."

And now I'd brought her up again!

"Well, you're interesting," I said. "And cool."

That stopped the conversation dead. We went back to hacking at the vines. We'd actually managed to cut through three, and were starting on a fourth, saying lame things like, "Three bittersweet down, ninety-eight billion more to go," when his cell phone rang.

"Hey, Dad." His voice was flat. "Yeah. . . . No, it's still going on. . . . No. . . . I don't know. Probably for a while. . . . Yeah. It's very worthwhile." He rolled his eyes at me. "I know. I'll be home as soon as it's done."

"He'd kill me if he saw me doing this," he said when he got off, squinching his face as he squeezed the clippers shut.

I kept sawing. "How come?"

"My hands. They're gonna be pretty stiff tomorrow."

"You have arthritis?" They didn't look like Mr. Horton's hands. They were long and pale, and very clean.

"Nah," he said. "The violin. I'm supposed to perform again tomorrow."

"So you must be a really fantastic violinist," I said.

"If I practiced more, maybe. Or practiced at all, according to him. And the reason he won't let me go to school, by the way, is because if I do, I won't be able to practice six hours a day under his helpful supervision. He works at home so he can"—he made a Westenburg-like face—"'be there for me.'"

"Like my mom!" I said. "That sounds exactly—"

"And I really do not want to play in that thing of his tomorrow. It's this extremely long and incredibly boring, like, variety show, called *Interest Day,* where every kid in the whole homeschool group, from age four on up, gets up and does something. But there's no way I can get out of it, because my mom and dad are like"—he did the Westenburg face again—"founding members, and my dad is Mr. Home-school Honcho."

Without thinking, I said, "My mom keeps pestering me to join a homeschool group with her."

He stopped clipping. "I thought you were already in a homeschool group. The Home—"

"Shut up!" I clamped my hand over his mouth but didn't look at him. "Just shut up, okay? Don't say it! It's too embarrassing. I don't know why . . . I just sort of . . ." My face burned as I tripped over my words. It didn't help that I could feel his mouth twitching under my hand, like it was dying to say something. I hardly breathed as I took my hand away. "There is no Homeschool Liberation League." Blood pounded in my ears as I waited for him to say, *Well, duh*.

Instead his eyes opened in mock surprise. "Isn't this it?" he said. "I mean, this is a secret meeting, right? With no last names, to protect our identities?"

"I can explain," I said. "No. No, I can't." I started sawing again. "You must think I'm the worst liar. You must totally hate me."

"Why?" he said. "It's great. Why do you think my dad let me go out this afternoon?"

I sneaked a glance at him. "You told him you were going to the Homeschool Liberation League?"

He shrugged innocently. "I told him it's a new group that's just starting up. I told him they were having a planning session, to work on the by-laws."

I felt like throwing my arms around him, but I still could hardly breathe for worry. "And what about Francesca? What'd you say to her when she told you?"

He shrugged again. "I told her I was the treasurer. I asked if she wanted to make a donation."

And then I did throw my arms around him.

No, I didn't. But I think he knew I wanted to.

18

"And does he feel the same way about you?" Alyssa asked.

"I think he does," I said. I'd called her house the minute I got home.

"I knew it! Told you!" Jess was there, on the other extension.

"But he's a friend too. We're friends," I said. "That's the coolest part!"

"Yeah, yeah. So did anything, you know . . . happen?" she asked.

"Yes! I mean, no! Not like that! But not *not* like that, if you know what I'm saying."

I was torn between wanting to hug the past few hours to myself, and replaying every detail for them. Except for the part about Francesca and the Homeschool Liberation League. That was my sweet secret. But I told them how I'd walked him home from the field, and then, when we were almost at his house, he decided to walk me back to my house, and when we got to the field again, the sunset was so beautiful that we stayed there till the stars came out.

"And what'd you talk about, lying on the grass together?" Jessie asked. "Please tell me not homeschool and funguses."

Mom knocked on my door to say they'd waited dinner. "I don't need dinner," I called back to her. "I'm not hungry. We were trying to figure out how to see each other," I answered Jessie. "He has two violin lessons a week in New Haven, and then chamber music on Tuesday nights, and he coaches little kids at his other homeschool group"—I loved being able to say "other homeschool group"—"Saturday mornings, plus recitals and concerts, and then of course he has to practice all the time. Plus his schoolwork. Plus, you know, I'm busy too."

I waited for her to say, *Right! At the salon!* But I was too happy to care about the salon now, or even the DIM.

"Guess you'll just have to sneak out in the night and meet in the field," Alyssa said.

"I know!" I said. "That's what I was thinking."

I was lying on my bed, later, still thinking about it, when my e-mail dinged. My heart leaped. I'd given Milo my e-mail! Or maybe it was Rosie, finally.

No, but it was someone almost as good: Dimitri.

✉ Katya, you asked for more ideas for more projects? From that list, I'd say you've got enough to keep you busy for years!

He went on to give me two screens' worth of info and suggestions, so detailed I couldn't get it all in one reading.

Who are you working with? he ended. Someone good, I hope.

No one, I wrote back. It's all *independent study.*

He replied almost instantly: So are you keeping careful notes and writing everything up?

Uh, not yet, I answered.

Gotta do it, K., he shot back. It's great to be interested in everything. Now you need to focus in and start being (I know, argh!) disciplined and (you should pardon the expression) systematic.

If I write something up, I answered, will you read it?

Sure. Hope I didn't throw too much at you, K. It's only coz I'm excited you're a *science person.*

Science person? I'd been floating in a fog of happiness all night. Now I was totally ecstatic. After printing out his e-mail to reread later, I Googled garlic mustard and found a bunch of scarily scientific but useful-looking articles. While they printed, I e-mailed Rosie again.

✉ GUESS WHAT!
I have a mentor . . . DIMITRI!!! And a new friend/possible boyfriend??? Who homeschools too. Would you like to join the Homeschool Liberation League?

Please answer. I miss you lots. Katya

Then I printed out a diagram of the human body with all its organs. Then I wanted to find out where kudzu came from. Japan, though I read that the Chinese had been using its roots for medicinal tea for thousands of years. Then I Googled Milo, who, I read, was a busy young prodigy who'd started violin at the age of four, played with many prestigious orchestras around the country, and was being home-schooled using an "accredited correspondence course." I even printed out a picture of him in a tuxedo.

Then I wrote to a plant biologist from one of the websites I'd found.

✉ Dear Dr. Zhang:
I am a thirteen-year-old homeschooler interested in the problem of invasive alien species. I saw a story on TV last night about vineyard owners using sheep to eradicate weeds, after first training them not to eat the grapes or vines. (After being fed the grapes/vines, they are given a dose of some drug that makes them nauseous. This teaches them to hate and avoid grapes.)

Do you think this could work the opposite way as well? Training sheep to eat invasive alien plants that they might otherwise not like, by teaching them to associate the bad plants with something good? What that is could be easily determined. If this would not work with sheep, it might with goats. Goats, from what I have read, will eat anything.

I am good with animals as well as plants. If you think this idea is worth pursuing and know anyone who raises sheep or goats, I would love to work on it, with you, or anyone.

By now I was so totally bubbling over, I hit SEND and went out to talk to Mom and Dad. Not about Milo, though I couldn't keep his name from creeping in a bunch of times, but about the experiment Dimitri had suggested to see if garlic mustard inhibited common garden vegetables. Dad thought that sounded great. He even offered to give me planters, and leftover seeds to plant in them alongside the garlic mustard.

"Just don't expect us to eat the stuff," Mom said.

Which gave me yet another idea.

Mr. Jeffrey Miller
Food Network
New York, NY

Dear Mr. Miller:
My parents are big fans of your network. They watch every night. But in my opinion, your shows have been getting kind of old.

Have you considered starting a show (with cookbook spinoff, of course!) using commonly found wild plants to make tasty meals? I'm thinking you could call it *Weed Feed.*

There are many reasons this is a good idea. 1) Wild food is free. 2) It can be humorous if/when some of the dishes turn out not to be that good, but 3) exciting when they are. 4) The wild food recipes I have found so far tend to be kind of bad, so there is a real need. 5) It can help solve a growing environmental problem that too few people know about: invasive alien plants replacing native species!

I have no suggestions yet for celebrity chefs. However, if you would like me to be a consultant on the show, or possibly be on it, I'd be very interested.

Sincerely,
Katya Antonucci

I was so pumped it didn't bother me a bit that I didn't see Milo that week. I did hear from him. Just silly IMs like, eradicated any evil enemies? and hope the HLL hasn't met without me, but enough of them to let me know that he was thinking of me. I worried a little about no reply from Rosie. I thought of just calling and saying, *Are you mad at me?* But with all that was going on, it didn't happen.

The salon, amazingly enough, seemed to be bothering me a little less too. So when some new client was taking forever Thursday afternoon, and Mom pulled me aside to ask if I'd help her out and do Mr. Horton's feet, I said, "Sure. No problem." I'd been waiting all week to tell him what I'd been doing. Just last night I'd read about something that could help with his arthritis.

Mom's client had a long face and a long nose and a long, graying ponytail. She'd come in asking for a new look. Mom had convinced her to go layered and try a golden blond tint, but the woman was having second thoughts, and third, and fourth. "Hold on, Donna!" she cried now as Mom pulled up a lock of hair to snip. "Are you sure bangs are the right idea for me? I don't mean to keep questioning your judgment, but . . ."

I caught Mom's eye in the mirror and shot her a *Well, then, don't, lady!* look.

She threw me a *Tell me about it!* look in return. "I don't want you to think bangs like old-fashioned bangs," she told the woman. "We're just going for a softer look around your face."

"Anything you can do for my face?" Mr. Horton said as he came in. His legs seemed much less rickety today, I was glad to see.

"Your face looks fine, Eddie," she said. "How's the rest of you doing?"

"Not too bad." He smiled at me. "Better, now that I'm here."

"Have you ever tried nettles for your arthritis?" I asked as he climbed onto the pedicure chair. "Because I read that if you put fresh leaves from the stinging nettle plant all over your—"

"Youch!" He shuddered. "Think I'll stick with the arthritis. Have you ever been stung by a nettle?"

"Uh . . ." I made a face. "Not really. I could look for other plant remedies, though, if you want." I un-Velcroed his sneakers and pulled off his socks. "There's gotta be something out there that will help." While the basin filled I told him about cutting down the bittersweet and pulling garlic mustard.

"Well, maybe you should try to find me a remedy," he said. "So I can go with you next time."

"Okay." I told him about digging up garlic mustard for the experiment and writing to the beaver expert. "He might be dead, though," I said, "because he published his squashed beaver article in like, nineteen fifty th—"

"I'm a little worried about the color," the client cut in. "You don't think it's a little brassy?"

"It's a lovely, soft color, Brooke." Mom threw me a *Dear God give me patience* look. "It's just wet now, that's all. You'll see when it's dry."

"Oh yeah, you're in good hands with Donna," Mr. Horton assured her. "She's gonna to make you look good, don't you worry. It's already very flattering." He put on his glasses so he could read the buttons on the chair's control panel. "Think I'll give myself the full massage treatment today. Neck, shoulders, spine, the works."

The client attempted a smile. "That sounds heavenly."

"And necessary," he said. "If I'm gonna keep up with Katya. How're the old dogs looking today, by the way?"

I could feel Mom watching as I carefully inspected his soles and heels and in between each toe. "Okay, I think."

I turned on the whirlpool and began washing his feet and legs, not with the usual scrubber, which was too rough to risk using on his feet, but with a soft sponge fresh from the sterilizer. I felt kind of weird peering up at him from my little stool, with a tray of creams and lotions next to me, and my hands in a bubbling tub of lavender-scented hot water. Especially with old Brooke watching everything in the mirror. But the way he kept beaming down at me, it was hard to totally hate it.

"Is the water hot enough?" I asked.

"Oh, yes! And with these massage gizmos working their magic . . ." He smiled over at Brooke. "You're right! I feel like I died and went to heaven!"

"Speaking of dying," I said. "Or not dying. I've also been reading about pancreases and dia—"

"You know, you're right," Brooke said to Mom. "I'm beginning to think this is going to look really nice."

How did Mom put up with this all day?

"You were saying, Katya?" Mr. Horton said.

His feet were starting to look pink and wrinkley, so I lifted each one from the water and wrapped them in a towel.

"Well, first of all, I found out what the pancreas is," I said. "Which I had no idea. It's a gland, which is basically an organ that secretes something for use somewhere in your body. I didn't know that either." I could see Mom watching us in the mirror too. It was amazing how much better she'd made the woman look. And how much less like a horse. "Did you know that's what a gland was, Mom?"

"Not really," she said. "I mean, I know glands swell up when you're sick. But that's about all."

"Well, it's like, six to eight inches long, your pancreas." Mr. Horton's feet seemed nice and dry now, so I rubbed

155

lotion on them as I talked. "It's right behind your stomach. And what it does is secrete pancreatic juices and insulin into your bloodstream. I'm not sure yet what the pancreatic juices do, but the insulin regulates the sugar and salt balance in your body." I looked up at him. "Which is why I'm talking about this. Those chips you were eating? The salt's bad for your blood pressure. They're also way too fattening. Overweight is a major risk factor with diabetes."

He made a face. "Uh-oh, Donna! I don't know if I want to hang out with this girl anymore. She knows too much."

"Sorry!" I said. "I don't mean to be obnoxious." While I pulled his socks over his knobby ankles, I told how I'd dug up six big healthy garlic mustard plants and sowed Dad's vegetable seeds around them, and now was waiting to see if the seeds would come up, or if the garlic mustard would stop them. "And did you know that there are these mycorrhizal fungi—I'm not how sure how you pronounce that—that live on the roots of plants and trees and help them grow?"

"Nope." He shook his head. "That's very interesting."

"I know!" I said. "And it's a chemical in the garlic mustard that inhibits the growth of the fungi. Which I assume means kills them. So I've been wondering what the chemical is, and if it possibly also inhibits, like, bad human funguses too. I'm wondering if anyone's looked into that. But I haven't figured out who to write to."

"And what are you going to do with all this information?" he asked.

"I don't know yet," I said. "Something."

I'd been noticing Brooke watching me in the mirror again. "She's a very bright girl," she told Mom. "How come she's not in school today?"

"I'm homeschooling her." Mom sometimes had an *And do you have a problem with that?* edge to her voice when she told clients. Not now. She seemed proud of me. Surprised, and really proud.

"Looks like she gives a great pedicure too." Brooke smiled over at Mr. Horton again. "Maybe I should get one. Since I seem to be getting a whole makeover today. That is, if she can take another client."

My stomach knotted. Mom wasn't really going to make me wash this woman's feet, was she?

Mom didn't answer. I tried to catch her eye, but she'd bent down to get the dryer.

She'd said it over and over to me, though: *This is a service business. Even when what the client asks for is ridiculous, you smile and find a way to please. That's what keeps them coming back.*

I didn't care if this lady came back. But Mom had to make a living. I knew that.

I held my breath. How long could it take someone to pull out the stupid dryer? And why wasn't she answering?

She had her suave, the-customer-is-always-right face on as she plugged it in. But her voice was stiff. "Kait . . Katya doesn't actually work here, Brooke. We're just using the salon as our homeschool headquarters at the moment." Her eyes flicked to me. "And she helps me out. And Eddie's her friend as well as my client. But if you'd like a pedicure, I'd be happy to give you one."

My breath whooshed out so loud, I was sure they heard.

"Well, that's an embarrassing mistake!" Brooke said. "I mean, I thought she looked a little young to be working in a . . . But you know, these days . . ."

So many looks flashed across Mom's face as she fiddled with the dryer, I couldn't tell what she was going to say next. For an instant there, I thought she was going to tell Brooke to leave, wet hair and all. But when she finally answered she seemed almost sad. "I can see why you'd think that," she said. "A lot of people make that mistake."

Mr. Horton had been doing up his shoes as if he wasn't listening. "You know," he said, "I've got tons of stuff at home about diabetes, Katya, if you're interested. I could probably scare up some something in one of my magazines about funguses too, if I look around. If your mom's not too busy to let you go, you could come back with me. We can stop off on the way, and see what your beaver friend is up to."

The look Mom gave me made my heart catch.

"Good idea," she said. "Go ahead, honey."

A wave of love washed over me. For Mom, but also for Mr. Horton, and for this woman too, for finally getting Mom to see.

"You know, that's a beautiful haircut, Mom," I said.

Things were going to change here now. I could feel it. If I didn't push too hard or piss her off, it was going to happen.

And then, to make a great day even better, after Mr. Horton loaded me up with books and magazines and drove me home, I called Milo. He didn't say, "Wanna meet me at the field?" the way I'd dreamed, but he asked me to come over Saturday.

CHAPTER 19

Milo's house wasn't in one of the new developments, like ours. It was a big old white farmhouse with green shutters, and a front and back porch, and too many doors to choose from.

"I was just taking a little practice break," he said as he opened the front door for me. "My eighty-eighth of the day. Your timing is perfect!" His hair looked like he'd just stepped out of the shower. His skin was pink and shiny, as if he'd just shaved. "You'll be sad to hear my dad's not home," he added with a wry face. "They're out shopping."

"Cool," I said, glad he didn't know how long I'd stood there trying to decide if I'd gone to the right door and picking stick-tights off my jeans. What I'd thought was a shortcut through the woods had ended in a giant thicket.

"Yeah, so . . . welcome. I guess the Homeschool Liberation League is now in session." He held out the bowl he was carrying. "Want some mac and cheese?"

I shook my head. "I gave up mac and cheese when I left school. I've almost given up pizza too, if you can believe that. Same reason."

I followed him into a very nice but cluttered living room with a grand piano and lots of bookcases and paintings, including a big one of a round-faced, maybe six-year-old, very earnest Milo in a suit, playing the violin. There were a bunch of framed photos of him on the piano too, but before I could check them out, he'd headed for the stairs.

"So this is really okay with you, keeping me company while I practice?" he said as we walked up. "I couldn't think of another way for us to get together. You probably want to be outside eradicating something, but my teacher's all over me for not practicing enough. Plus, I got invited to play quartets on Sunday with some guys from the New Haven Symphony, so I need to learn my parts." He looked almost as earnest as in the portrait, but more nervous.

Which made me more nervous.

"It's fine," I said. "It's really fine. It's more than fine. I'm mean, if it's fine with you."

I'm not sure what I'd expected his room to be like. Music strewn everywhere, maybe, a heap of patchwork pajamas on the floor, posters of famous violinists? It was neater than mine, as it turned out, with a made bed, a red beanbag chair, an only slightly messy desk, a tall music stand, and a wall of colored-pencil drawings—clearly done by him, I hoped not recently—of your basic fearsome robots.

"Sit anywhere you want," he said, taking a last bite of mac and cheese before putting the bowl down on his desk and wiping his hands on a towel. "Hope you brought something to read."

"No." I looked at the books overflowing his bookcases, lots clearly for schoolwork, but graphic novels too, and science fiction and fantasy. "But that's fine."

Vowing not to say "fine" again for the rest of my life, I settled myself in the beanbag chair with a few fantasy novels. But as soon as he started playing, I knew I wasn't reading. Not that he was playing a piece, just little snatches, over and over, first slowly, then faster, sometimes clearly pleased with what he heard, other times cursing. But even when he seemed to hate it, the sounds coming out of the violin had this brilliance to them. Like sunlight. Like he was an extension of the violin or the violin was an extension of him. Or something. I don't know what the words are for stuff like that, any more than I can describe the sounds, or the look on his face. I only know that as he leaned into the music, swayed with it, went up on tiptoes at the high notes, that wiry, frowning, ironic awkwardness about him was completely gone. And I didn't care at all that he was paying no attention to me. It felt so good that both of us had this thing we loved: me, bashing around to find out things, him his music. Which sounds as yuckily pretentious as saying that time stopped for me. Or that the music pierced my heart. Or that I didn't know someone's wrist could be so beautiful. But that's what I was feeling, listening to him. For an hour, at least. Which was pretty amazing for me.

But then my foot fell asleep. And then I had to go to the bathroom. And then, after finding the bathroom and looking at enough books out in the hall to determine that his mom was a lawyer and his dad a mathematician, or vice versa, my stomach started growling, and I decided Milo wouldn't mind if I ate the rest of his mac and cheese. His eyes flicked to me each time I got up. But he kept playing. And I kept listening for another long time before I started reading.

I'd read almost half of some book set in the kingdom of Sothoii when he stopped playing and came over to me.

His eyes were sparkling. "Your turn," he said.

"For what?"

He looked at me like, *Duh!* "A violin lesson."

My heart jumped. "Me? I'm not a music person."

"Not yet." He put the violin down and pulled me to my feet. "Come on. It'll be fun. Plus, I told my folks that's why you were coming over, and they'll be back soon. You play an instrument, right?"

I'd never seen him so animated.

I wrinkled my nose. "Just flute and piccolo. And not too well."

"Doesn't matter." He picked up the violin again and put it under his chin. "See how I'm holding it, resting the violin on my left shoulder, with my chin resting on the chin rest, and the neck—this long part is the neck—resting between my thumb and first finger. Oops, that's four 'rests' in one sentence. See, I need a rest!" He handed me the violin.

I held on tight, but my palms were sweating. "What if I drop it?"

"I'll never have to play again? Don't worry. You won't drop it. Anyway, it's insured."

"Okay." I raised the violin to my shoulder and put my chin on the chin rest. I got an instant crick in my neck, but I didn't say anything. "Now what?"

He adjusted my hand. "Relax your wrist. Don't let your palm rest against the neck. And you don't have to clutch it for dear life."

I didn't mean to giggle, but as he put a hand on my shoulder, one escaped.

"Relax," he said.

Relax? When he was standing so close I could count his eyelashes?

"And breathe. You can't play when you're holding your breath. Not that it ever helps when people tell me that. Now try plucking the strings with your right hand, just to see what it sounds like."

Gingerly, I ran a finger across each of the four strings, then, when no sound came out, plucked harder. It wasn't a nice sound, but it was definitely a sound.

"Is that right?" I looked up at him.

"Yeah. Do it again."

I kept plucking till the sound got clearer. "Now how do I make notes?"

He explained how the pitch changed depending on where you put the fingers of your left hand on the string.

"Like pressing the keys on the flute," I said.

He grinned. "Exactly! You're a genius. See, I knew you'd like this. Try it."

This close to me, he felt taller than I'd remembered. I

looked up at him again. "Okay, but I don't get how you do one thing with one hand and something else with the other."

"I'll help you." He reached over for his bow, then moved behind me and, circling me with his arms, positioned my left hand with his. "You need to press the string down to the fingerboard," he said, putting his fingers lightly over mine and pushing each one down in turn. "Firm, but not like, death grip, right? This string you're playing now, the lowest string, is G."

If I'd found it hard to breathe before, I totally wasn't breathing now. I could feel his breath on my neck, and his body, not touching mine, but close. So close it was like the air between us was humming.

"Let's ease your hand over one string, to the D," he said, moving it for me. "For now just rest it a tiny bit above the string, but not touching. I'll tell you what finger to press down, okay? But not yet. I'm gonna play two open strings first. Two Gs, two Ds, and then you're on. Ready?" I couldn't see his face, but his voice told me he was smiling. "Here we go."

But when he drew the bow across the string, it was so loud I jumped, which made us both laugh, and he had to adjust my hand again.

"'Twinkle, Twinkle,' take two!" he called.

"We're playing 'Twinkle, Twinkle'?" I twisted around to see his face, totally messing up my hand position again. But he got it fixed, and with him calling out instructions, and pressing my fingers down for me, by take six I started to get the idea.

"I'm playing the violin!" I cried. Or crowed. My voice

wasn't totally in my control. "You're right! This is so fun! I love it!"

"I knew you would," he said. "So . . . those times you heard me playing out on the field? You must have thought I was nuts."

"What made you think of that?" I asked. "Is that what I sound like now?"

"No." He took the violin from me.

It was a relief to be able to straighten my neck. But now we were face-to-face again. It suddenly felt embarrassing.

"I was upset about someone," he said. "Who was totally not worth it."

I nodded. "I know what you mean."

He seemed to be staring at my lips. Which made me super conscious of them.

"You were right to change your name to Katya," he said.

My throat tightened. "What do you mean?"

"Francesca called you Kaitlyn or Kaity a few times when she talked to me, but you don't look like a Kaitlyn. You're definitely not a Kaity."

My lips felt like those plastic Halloween lips, or those pooched-out ones in lipstick commercials. "What does a Kaity look like?"

"More like, you know . . . cute."

They were, in fact, tingling now. "Excuse me. I'm not cute?" I pretended to be outraged.

"Uh-uh." He was still staring at them. "You're too weird to be cute."

166

Could I tell him I'd had the exact same thought about him?

"I mean look at your hair." He reached out and pulled a stick from it. "It's like it should have bittersweet berries and spotted knapweed stuck in it. I'm not saying geeky can't be beautiful—"

"Geeky?" I shouted, even as the "beautiful" made my heart stop. "With invasive alien twigs in my hair? Should it have sea squirts stuck in it too?"

"Not stuck in it like they *got* stuck in it," he said. "Like someone stuck them there on purpose. To look beautiful. Which they would. On you. Which you do." I was totally blushing now, and he looked totally embarrassed. Not too embarrassed to be still staring at my mouth, though. He moved a little closer. "Really. Geeky's good," he said. "I like geeky."

"Good thing," I shot back, my eyes on his mouth too as I touched one of the short clumps on the side of his head. It felt as smooth and silky as it looked. "Because look at your hair. It's like a horse bit off chunks of it."

"Yeah, well, it keeps flopping in my face when I'm playing. So when a piece annoys me, I cut it off. Now you're gonna ask me why I don't just cut it all off, right?"

"No," I said. "It works perfectly with your geeky pajamas."

If it had been hard to breathe with him standing behind me, it was almost impossible with his eyes on my lips.

I was thinking that if he didn't put the stupid violin

167

down and make his move soon, I would, when the door opened.

Light glinted off his dad's wire-rimmed glasses as he stood in the doorway. "I was just wondering how your practicing is going," he said as we jumped apart. "What I heard sounded more like 'Twinkle, Twinkle.'"

"I was giving Katya a violin lesson," Milo said.

"I have no problem with that," his dad said, looking me over the same way he did in the Dutch Treat. "I'd just like to remind you that tomorrow—"

"I know, Dad." There was an edge to Milo's voice. "You don't have to remind me."

"Evidently I do," his dad said.

I could see now where Milo had gotten his raised eyebrow trick. Except that no matter how dry and sarcastic Milo was being, I could always feel the humor behind it. His dad seemed about as humorous as poison ivy. But then he turned to me, and with what he clearly meant to be a smile, said, "I'm sorry to cut this short, Katya. I don't know if Milo told you, but he's got a lot of important things pending at the moment. I'm Preston Mathias, by the way." He stuck out his hand for me to shake and, with another raise of his eyebrow added, "The evil dad."

"Dad!" Milo looked like he wanted to sink through the floor.

"So, Milo tells me you've joined the world of homeschooling. That's great!" his dad said as, mortified for Milo but not wanting to be rude, I went over and shook his hand. He didn't just give one shake and let go either; he held on and kept shaking, telling me how great it was. His eyes were a pale blue, not round and dark, like Milo's, but they were just as intense. "Our homeschool group is always looking for new members. We'd be delighted to have you and your folks join. Milo can give you the particulars—"

"Dad!"

No, not sink through the floor. Pound his father through it.

"I should go," I said.

Milo shot me a look. "But you're coming back Monday morning, right?" he said. "With your schoolwork. So you can study while I practice. And have another lesson."

"Uh, yeah," I said, though it was the first I'd heard of it.

"Or . . ." He stared defiantly at his dad. "Maybe I'll do my practicing at your house next time.

"And you wondered why I want to go to school?" he said a minute later as he walked me to the road. "I was serious about Monday," he added. He looked shy, suddenly. "If you really don't mind listening to me practice, and you think it can work for you. Because it worked really well for me, in case you couldn't tell."

I nodded. "Me too." I was already planning what I'd say to Mom, who, I thought, might actually say yes. We hadn't talked more about my life after that amazing turning point in the salon the other day, but . . .

"Good thing," Milo said. He reached out and pulled me to him, and, so fast it was over before my body had gotten used to the idea, gave me the kiss I'd been waiting for.

20

I was still flying when I got home.

I'd been at Milo's so long, Mom had finished work and was out in the vegetable garden with Dad. They must have heard there was going to be a freeze tonight; they were picking all the tomatoes.

"Mom, remember how you told that Brooke lady I didn't work in the salon, I just helped you sometimes?" I broke off a stem of cherry tomatoes for myself as I hurried over to them. "Well, do you think we can change my schedule?" Juice shot all over me as I bit a tomato off the stem. I ate another, this time putting the whole thing in my mouth so it wouldn't squirt. "Because Milo just asked me to bring work over to his house Monday, for, like, a study date, except it won't be a date because we'd really be studying. Or I will. He'll be practicing. I can do the DIM assignments there just as easily as here." I bit off another tomato. "And we might need to get me a violin, because he's giving me violin lessons. You won't believe what a great violinist he is, and an amazing teacher. I've already started learning 'Twinkle, Twinkle'!"

Dad stood up and turned over an empty milk crate for me. "Sit down, honey." He had that family conference look in his eyes—not a good sign. "We've been wanting to talk to you too."

"Don't worry," I assured him. "His dad works at home. We won't be alone. Or we could work here, if that's better."

"It's not Milo, sweetie," Mom said. I didn't like the way she looked either. Not angry, just really serious. As if someone might have died serious. "We're glad you met someone nice."

I ate another tomato, but I barely tasted it.

"And if you want to take up the violin, that's great," Dad added. "But you mentioned what happened in the salon the other day. Your mother and I have been doing a lot of talking about that too."

"It's made us think about what we're doing," Mom said. "Which I thought I felt okay about . . . I wanted to feel okay about . . . but it was a real wake-up call for—"

"But that's good!" I said. "It's—"

Dad motioned again for me to sit. I sat. "Let her talk."

"You're too intelligent for us to be muddling along like this, Kaity," Mom said. "You've got too much going for you to be shut up in the salon with me trying to teach you. Much as I've liked having you around, it's not right. And it's not the education you need. I don't want to wake up five years from now and find out we made the wrong decision and you can't do what you need to with your life because we were shortsighted."

171

This wasn't how Mom talked. It sounded like a speech she'd been practicing.

"But that's good," I tried again. "Don't take this wrong, Mom, but you needed a wake-up call. I know you hate the word *unschooling*, but I've got a real study plan now, and lots more materials, and Milo's got a ton of excellent schoolbooks"—I was winging it here—"from this like, accredited correspondence course, and I know he'd . . ."

Dad pulled his crate in closer to me. "Listen to me, Kaity," he said as Mom pulled hers closer too. "I know how much you've wanted this to work. And I know this isn't what you want to hear. We've given it our best shot for a month now. It's time for you to go back."

"To school?" I felt like I'd been blasted by a fire hose. "This is a joke, right?" I could see from their faces that it wasn't, but I said it again. "You're joking. What about all those things you said when we were weeding, Dad? About my dreams?"

"Why do you think I'm saying this?" he said. "You need to be with people who can stimulate you and guide you. Point you in directions you don't know about, and we have no clue about."

"Exactly!" I said. "Which is why I'm not muddling along, even if you are! Which is why I want to change how we're doing it. That's what Mom's saying too, aren't you Mom? But that doesn't mean going back to—"

"I mean, I read all these homeschool moms' blogs," she said. "About the things they're researching, and the other moms they're corresponding with, and the great places they're taking them and the fantastic opportunities they're finding for them. I mean, maybe if Dad or I could quit our job, or even take a few months off to—"

"You don't have to," I said. "I have Dimitri, who's going to read anything I write. I have Mr. Horton and his collection. And I wrote to a bunch of scientists—"

"And that's great, Kaity," Dad said. "But it's not a plan. It's more like, I don't know, Waffle when we get him home from the kennel. Medicinal plants, wow! Beavers, great! Coyotes, invasive weeds, violin, lemme at it! You're all over the map, honey."

"Because I've got interests! Which I never had! My brain was dead. I didn't even want a brain. And now it's finally coming back to life and you're comparing me to Waffle?"

Waffle, hearing his name, came out from under the zucchini plant where he'd been sleeping, and with a worried look, stuck his nose in my hand.

"Don't get me wrong," Dad said. "We love that you've got these interests. But you don't even know yet what else you might be interested in, that you'll never get to find out about at home. You're thirteen years old, honey. You need guidance with all this enthusiasm. And structure, and support, and a grounding in the fundamentals—"

"Not to mention that the salon feels like jail to you," Mom said. "And I don't blame you. God knows, it feels like that to me too sometimes."

"Which is why I'm asking to go to Milo's. And have him

come here. Or work out something else. Please, Mom. I didn't belong at school before I started this. I totally couldn't belong there now!" I felt a knot of tears forming. "Do you know what will happen to me if I go back there? Do you know what they'll turn me into?"

"I don't think you need to worry about that," Mom said. "You said yourself you've got Dimitri, and Eddie Horton. And you've got Milo now—"

"Who I won't have time to see—"

"And you know Alyssa and Jessie will be thrilled to have you ba—"

"Yes, but I'm not like them any—"

"And there's your friend Francesca. She called this afternoon to see if you'd come visit her in the hospital."

"What?" I jumped up so fast I knocked over the milk crate.

"The girl with the appendicitis?" Dad looked at Mom. "Her operation was last week. She's still in the hospital?"

"Yeah," Mom said. "She picked up some really bad infection. She sounded terrible. I felt so sorry for her, I told her we'd run Kaity down to New Haven tomorrow for a visit."

My mind jumped to all the stuff I'd skimmed over when I looked up appendicitis. The scary stuff, about things that could go wrong. And the pictures. But I couldn't think about that now. "You're sending me back to school and taking me to see Francesca? Why don't you just dig a hole right here, while you're at it, and I'll jump in and you can throw dirt on me! And stop calling me Kaity. I am not Kaity!"

Waffle, upset that I was yelling, barked.

Mom pulled out a cigarette. Dad gave her a look but didn't say anything. She put it in her mouth but didn't light it.

"They've got a new teacher in the Resource Room," she said. "A retired science teacher. They can arrange your schedule so she works with you a full period every day. I thought we could go in and meet her. And they have a very nice new counselor at school, Dr. Gordon—"

"You talked to the counselor? Don't tell me you talked to Westenburg too? Behind my back?"

"We were just exploring honey," Dad said. "It was informal. We told him all the really original and creative things you're—"

"We were surprised how open he was," Mom said.

"Yeah. I'm sure he loved having you come crawling back!"

"Nobody's crawling," Dad said. "It's not a defeat, honey. And Westenburg's not the point. It's not about Westenburg. It's about you, and not letting you down."

"What happens to my projects, and my violin lessons, and my study sessions?"

"You can still do all that," Mom said. "You'll just do it on weekends. And after school."

"Right," I said. "After I finish my mind-numbing homework and come out of my coma from being bored out of my skull. If I do. If I don't, I can drop out and work in a beauty parlor."

She looked like I'd punched her.

The words hung in the air, picking up more meanness with every second.

I'd have grabbed them back if I could. Or tried to undo them.

But then Dad said, "Watch your step, young lady. That's not going to help." As if I was some bad little girl. And I heard myself say, "So I'm just going back to school Monday. That's it. You've decided. I can just kiss my dreams good-bye."

His face was like, *Case closed*. "We're doing what we think is best."

CHAPTER 21

I didn't know you could hate anyone as much as I hated them.

After I'd stopped crying, I tried calling Milo. He didn't pick up his cell, and when I called his house, his dad said he was practicing. So I called the only other person I knew would understand: Rosie.

"I know you're probably mad at me for not writing for so long," I told her voice mail. "But I really need to talk to you. Something really bad has—"

"Katya?" Her voice came on the line, surprised but friendly. "Hey. What's going on?"

The lump in my throat was so big, it was hard to talk. "They're making me go back to school," I said. "I don't know what to do."

"But it was going so great," she said. "What happened?

"Well," she said when I finished telling her. "You want to hear something funny? I'm back at school too. I started high school."

"What?" I was so startled, I had to sit. "Who made you? I thought your moms—"

"No one made me." She sounded sheepish suddenly. "It was my idea. You see, our high school is really pretty good. And I love my moms, but it was getting a little intense around here, and . . ." Her reasons rolled on: drama club . . . jazz chorus . . . amazing conductor . . . travels all over performing . . . we're this . . . we're that . . .

I couldn't listen. "Well, that all sounds fine," I said, trying to keep my voice from trembling. "Except now you have to be in school."

"I know." She sounded even more sheepish. "I kind of like it. And if I stop liking it, I can apply to this college called Simon's Rock, which lets you start after tenth grade. I know a bunch of kids who've done that. Or our community college will let me take . . ." She must have realized I'd stopped listening again. "I'm sorry I didn't tell you, Katya. It's just, all that stuff you said about how I was your inspiration and your role model, I felt kind of weird. Plus, there's been so much going on at school. But I'm really glad you called now."

I'd been scribbling in my Discovery Journal while she talked, covering the page with spirals and more spirals, until my notes, and the heading TO TELL DIMITRI, looked like they'd been swallowed up by a giant black hairball.

"So does that mean you won't be going to camp this summer either?" I asked.

"Uh . . . I'm not sure," she said. "I mean, if the chorus goes to China . . ."

That wasn't the end of the conversation. She wanted to

know about Milo. But I felt like we were on different continents, with an ocean between us. And when I got off, except for some vague promises to stay in touch, I couldn't remember what we'd said.

"Katya, honey, you all right?" Dad called through the door at some point. "Listen, we can go to the Peabody Museum tomorrow before the hospital if you want. I know you've been wanting to. Or we could go to Pepe's for a pizza. Or both."

Oh, so now he was being nice to me?

"I'm not going," I said.

"Mom's already called Francesca's mom," he said. "She's really sick, honey. We can't disappoint her."

Alyssa texted me: long time no hear. wassup? have u seen M????

Mr. Horton e-mailed: I was thinking about going for a drive first thing tomorrow morning. Sunrise is at 6:44. Care to join me?

I didn't answer anyone.

It was past ten when Milo finally called.

"I have to get out of here," I said almost before he said hello. "Can you meet me at the field?"

"Now?" The way he said it made my throat clench. "I'm still kind of practicing. It's started going so well I can hardly believe it. Ever since you came over, Katya . . . It's like something great happened when you were here with me. It's like

I had this breakthrough. What's up?" He said it the way people do when they're hoping you'll say "Nothing much," so they can get off the phone. "You sound a little upset."

"A little upset?" I said. "Today might have been the last meeting of the Homeschool Liberation League, that's all. They're making me go back to school. On Monday. The good news is I won't have to worry about Francesca writing the article. She'll have nothing to write about. Wait, that's not true." I put on a news announcer voice: "Homeschool experiment fails. Antonucci bombs out. Parents pull the plug."

He cursed. "Oh, man! That sucks! But listen . . . Katya"—he sounded as uncomfortable as Rosie—"I want to hear about this, I really do, but . . . would it be okay if I call you back in, like, a few hours? Is that too late? I don't think I'll work past midnight. I've got the first movement almost down, and if I put in a couple more hours, I think I'll be in okay shape for tomorrow." He went on about the amazingness of his breakthrough and the excellence of the musicians he was going to play with. I was too upset to listen. "Are you mad at me?" he said when he finally caught on. "You sound mad."

"No," I said. "I'm not mad."

I felt like a hole had opened in my heart when I hung up. By the time midnight came I didn't trust myself to talk even if he called back. I turned off my phone and got into bed. Thirty-two hours till school. Not even that till Francesca.

To keep from thinking about school, I tried picturing

myself marching into the hospital, announcing, "Well, you can stop worrying about being too sick to write about me, Francesca. There's nothing to write about now. It's over. Case closed. Finito."

Except there was no way that would end it. "Antonucci Bombs Out" was too juicy a story, way better than "The Wonders of Homeschool." She'd pounce all over that story.

Unless I came up with some other lie. Or she died in the night.

My skin prickled as I thought, What if she really is dying?

The answer rushed in: Yes, but then I won't have to face her tomorrow!

And then I felt sick.

It was one thing wanting to be someone new. But if this was the new me, I felt like flushing her down the toilet.

22

I'd only been in a hospital once before, when Grandpa had his gallbladder taken out. What I mostly remembered, aside from how short the hospital gown was, and how skinny his legs looked sticking out from under it, was the nursing station counter, covered with vases of flowers that Aunt Angie said came from the rooms of patients who'd died. "Not died," Mom had scolded her. "Went home."

Okay, there's no reason to think Francesca's dying, I told myself as I took the elevator to her floor. Being a horrible person with horrible thoughts doesn't make the horrible things happen. More likely she was sitting up in bed, surrounded by balloons and flowers from all her friends. She probably had friends here right now. In which case, I could say hi and stand there for a while, and leave.

"Nuuurse!" a moaning cry echoed down the hall. "Nuuuurse! Nuuuuuuurse!"

A man in a blue blazer walked by pushing a stretcher. The old lady in it looked so flat, it was like she had no body.

I wished I'd said yes when Mom offered to come up with me.

I was eyeing the emergency exit down the hall—wondering if I ducked in, ate the Godivas we'd bought for Francesca, and then took the stairs back down to the lobby, if I'd get locked in the stairwell—when my stomach dropped. Francesca was coming around the corner, pushing a metal pole on wheels with a limp red balloon tied to it, her mouth set in a grim line as she took slow, old-lady steps. The pole had bags with tubes hanging off it. She was only wearing one sleeve of her froufy, puff-sleeved robe, because the tubes were attached to her arm.

"Don't look at my hair," she said, shuffling along in her blue paper slippers. "Or the robe. My grandmother got it for me. She's stopping by later."

Her hair looked fine, I thought. It was her eyes that looked bad. Instead of their usual bright, snappy, miss-nothing blue, they were a weird combination of glittery and dull.

An aide pushing a cart flashed her a smile. "Hey, Frannie, didn't I just see you coming around the other way? What are you, training for the marathon?"

"Hey, Robert." Francesca managed a weak smile back at him. "I'm supposed to do twenty times around the nurses' station twice a day to build up my strength," she told me. "Wanna walk with me?"

"Sure." I fell in alongside her, taking tiny steps like hers, sneaking glances at her when she wasn't looking.

"I thought you said you were going home yesterday, Frannie," a woman coming out of a room called as we trudged by.

"I was supposed to," she said. "They changed their minds.

How're you doing today, Mrs. Brown?" As we walked on, she said under her breath, "I keep trying to tell people my name's not—"

"So you're not, like, dying or anything?" It popped out before I could stop myself.

"Only of boredom," she said. "And Jell-O. That's all they let me eat for days, orange Jell-O. Now I can have Cream of Wheat and soft-boiled eggs and mashed potatoes. Yippee, right? And I had all these visitors at first, but we're down to relatives now . . ."

"So then, you'll get better?"

She nodded. "Yeah, just not fast enough."

More people waved and said hello to her. She seemed to know everybody's name.

"So then . . . when they do let you out?" I started as we rounded the nurses' station again. "How long before you can go back to school? Do you know yet?" She shook her head. "But . . . have you been feeling well enough to like, work on . . ."

"The article?" She seemed embarrassed. "No. And I know I should be. I mean, it's totally overdue. But honestly? I haven't been thinking about anything but getting out of here. And eating food." She eyed the Godiva box with a look that reminded me of Waffle. "Not to be rude or anything, but is that for me?"

"Oh, sorry. Yeah." I handed it to her.

"Chocolates count as soft food, right, don't you—" Her eyes flicked to a gray-haired doctor coming down the hall.

"Uh-oh!" She grabbed my arm. "We'd better take it to the solarium."

A patient in blue sweats was slumped in an armchair watching the playoffs when we got there. He didn't look up when we came in. The minute we'd settled into the couch and she'd gotten her tubes untangled, she ripped the box open.

"You sure this is okay?" I said, remembering those drawings of intestinal tracts I'd been looking at online, picturing a Godiva stuck halfway down. "I don't think death by chocolate is supposed to mean you literally—"

"Want one?" She held out the box to me. I shook my head.

She'd barely popped the first one into her mouth when a beep like a loud car alarm went off. I jumped.

"It's just telling us the bag's empty." She laughed, stood up, and pressed the buttons on the box at the top of the pole until it stopped. "You thought it was the candy police?"

"I don't know what I thought," I said. "I'm a little tense."

"Yeah, well, I'm so glad you came," she said, eating another. "I mean, all these kids from school came to see me last week, kids I supposedly like"—she named the most popular kids in our grade—"and I'm like, go away, I don't want company, I am so not up to being perky and pleasant for you! Except I can't say that, so I have to put on my perky, pleasant smile and . . ." Her eyes suddenly turned serious. "Do you know what I'm saying, Katya?"

I nodded, though it was hard to believe Francesca was actually calling herself perky.

"I mean, I just get so sick of everyone constantly saying what a great sport I am. I mean, could I just be me once in a while? Would that kill people?" She gave me another searching look. "Is it okay that I'm telling you this? I don't mean to be complaining. You don't care that I'm not all perky, do you?"

My stomach jumped as I felt the sudden urge to say, *Not if you don't care that everything I told you was a lie.*

"Want some water?" I said. "I think I'm gonna get some water." When she shook her head, I got up and went over to the cooler in the corner and filled a cup for myself. Then, from across the room, before I could change my mind, I said, "Speaking of school, when you do go back, you're in for a surprise. My parents are making me go back there. Tomorrow."

"To MVB?" Her hand stopped halfway to the candy box. "No! What happened? I mean, it was going so great."

"Yeah, well . . ." I gulped down the cup of water. "They think it's gonna ruin my life. They think I need structure and guidance. In other words, they can't handle it."

"And you just gave up?" She looked worried. "You said yes? You can't do that! That's so not fair!"

Part of me felt like crying. The other part was like, *Okay. Here we go.*

"Well, I know it messes up part one of your series."

I held my breath.

"It's not that," she said. "I mean, it partly is. But what

happens to all those amazing things you're doing? I mean, you're obviously doing what's right for you. For you, school's obviously not right."

I did cry then. But I bent over and got myself more water and I don't think she saw.

She looked genuinely upset, though. "I'm really sorry, Kaity."

I came back to the couch and sat down again.

"You think I don't understand why you don't want to be there?" she said. "You think I really don't know all the ways school sucks?"

"I thought you loved school," I said. "You're Francesca Halloran, star of everything. Teachers love you, kids love you. Everyone wants to be you. You always have that sparkly, sprightly, spunky, everything is so fun and easy and interesting, I-live-for-school . . . You always know what you're doing—"

Her look reminded me of Milo. "Did you hear anything I said before? That doesn't mean I like it. I'm just good at it. It's a game, Katya. So I play to win, okay? I'm so good at playing it, most of the time I don't even know it is a game." Her eyes shone with feeling. "But you said no. I'm not playing. I can't do it. I really admire that."

I felt a horrible prickling in my nose again. "Yeah, well, you wouldn't if . . ."

Before I could say more, she held out the box. "Here. Eat the hazelnut ones. They're the best. And I'm not allowed to eat nuts."

I shook my head, but took one anyway.

"So we need to talk about what you're going to do," she said after we'd both eaten a bunch.

"Do?" I said. "What can I do?"

"I don't know," she said. "But I know you, Kaity. You're exactly like me. You always have an idea. You'll think of something."

"By tomorrow? Like what? Lock myself in my room? Run away?" I told her about Rosie, and my plan to move to her house when all this started. "But I can't even do that anymore." I told her about Rosie going back to school. I couldn't believe I was saying this to her. Or that she seemed to be getting it. I took a deep breath, then asked what I'd wanted to ask from the minute I got there. "If I do go back? You're not going to write about how I bombed out, are you?"

She looked insulted. "I would never do that. Why would I do that? Unless . . ." A gleam came into her eye. She sat up straighter. "What if you asked your parents for like, a few more weeks, and I wrote the article and did a really great job, and everyone got to read how about all the amazing things you're doing . . . could that work?"

"For you, yeah," I said.

"No, I meant for you. I mean, what if teachers like Mr. Z., who really likes you, by the way, read it and called your parents, and kids told their parents how what you're doing is so much more advanced and interesting and useful than what they're doing—I could get some kids to do that—and their parents ran into yours at, like, the Stop 'n' Shop, or in your mom's salon, and they were all like—"

I saw a flash of the old gung-ho Francesca.

"You're forgetting something," I said. "You're too sick to do it, and tomorrow's Monday."

"I know, but I'm really starting to feel better. And you could help me if you want. Or if you want, you can write the whole thing. Come on, it's a great idea, Katya."

My head was swimming. I wanted to ask if she'd always felt like that about school. I wondered if maybe we really were alike, and what that meant. I wondered if I should confess I lied.

"I already tried writing something like that," I said. "It's how I talked them into it in the first place. I can write till I'm blue in the face. The only thing that will change their minds is if, like, God, or Mr. Westenburg, tells them to." An electric jolt went through me. "I do have an idea," I said.

"I knew it!" Her eyes lit up. "Tell me!"

"Not yet. Let me call him first."

"Who?"

"Milo."

23

The good news was he was still in New Haven. His quartet rehearsal had just finished. Even better, he didn't sound mad at me for last night.

The bad news was he thought it was the worst idea he'd ever heard.

"Why?" I tried to sound calm and reasonable. "You said yourself he was Mr. Homeschool Honcho. Who better to talk to them about homeschooling?"

"Totally!" Francesca chimed in. "He knows everything about it!" She was watching out the solarium windows to make sure no one saw me using my cell. "When I called about the article that time, I could hardly get his dad off the phone!"

"Come on, Milo," I said. "If anyone can talk sense into them, it's your dad."

"Does he know it's now or never?" Francesca said. "Does he understand it's his dad or school?"

I motioned her to shut up so I could hear Milo. "My dad gets you in his clutches," he was saying, "you can kiss your life good-bye."

The word *kiss* made my heart leap. "But d'you think he'll meet us? My folks are in the hospital cafeteria, waiting for me. Where's he?"

"Here with me," he said flatly. "Where else?"

"Perfect!" I gave Francesca a thumbs-up.

"No," he said. "Perfect would be to keep him out of . . . you know . . . you and me."

"I know." My heart leaped again. "But you'll ask him? Please, Milo? And if he says yes, I'll call my mom right now. If they say yes, we'll meet you. Anywhere you want."

Half an hour later, the five of us met up in a dark, old-timey New Haven coffeehouse.

My nerves felt like I'd already had eighteen cups of coffee.

"So how'd the music go?" I asked Milo after we'd gotten through the intros and lame chitchat. I'd tried to sit next to him, but the parents outmaneuvered me.

"Oh, it went very well!" Preston stretched his arm across the top of the booth behind Milo. "They're terrific musicians!"

Maybe it was wishful thinking, but he didn't seem as mean and pompous as I remembered. Even his little wire-rimmed glasses and square-cut, no-mustache beard seemed less crabby cartoon sea captain, more professor-like. "That's great!" I said.

"Milo was playing string quartets," he told Mom and Dad, "with members of the New Haven Symphony."

Milo slid low enough in his seat that Preston's arm wasn't touching him and threw me a *Can I leave yet?* look.

"It was just for fun," he muttered.

"Yes, but he acquitted himself beautifully," his dad said. "I was very proud."

"I bet," my dad said. I could almost see him thinking, *Not our kind of guy.*

Mom seemed more interested in checking out Milo. Was that why she'd agreed to this? I wondered. So they could get a look at him? Or were they having second thoughts? After the horribleness of our fight yesterday, even the tiniest second thoughts were better than I'd expected. I threw Milo a *How do you think we're doing?* look, and got an eye-rolling shrug in return. I wished I could find his hand under the table without being noticed. "Thank you for doing this," I mouthed.

The waiter came and took our orders. The last thing I needed was caffeine, but when Milo ordered a latte, I said, "Same for me."

"So, Preston," Dad said once that was out of the way. "Kaitlyn tells us you're a homeschool expert." He draped his arm behind me too, and with an apologetic face at me, added, "Sorry, honey, I meant Katya. Anyway, Katya seems to think talking to you might change our minds about sending her back to school. But frankly"—he looked at me again—"I think that ship has sailed." Before I could get out a *Yes, but* . . . he'd launched into his whole "no structure," "all over the map," "her life will be ruined forever" thing.

"I hear what you're saying, Joe," Preston said as the waiter brought our coffees. He removed his arm from around Milo to squeeze the twist of lemon peel over his double espresso. "And I don't want you to think I'm one of those government-school-is-evil, homeschool-is-good, my-way-or-the-highway types. I'm a firm believer in public schools." He stirred it with the tiny spoon and looked over the tops of his glasses at Mom and Dad. "But I also believe that for the right families, homeschooling can be an excellent thing. In our case"—his eyes warmed as they moved to Milo—"it was clear early on that the usual path wouldn't do. We've homeschooled both Milo and his sister, Chloe, all the way through. With the help, of course, of our homeschool group, which my wife and I founded."

"Hey, that sounds like an expert to me!" I tried to smile without seeming like I was sucking up. "And as you know, Preston, the usual path isn't working for me either." Oh, argh! I sounded as stiff and pompous as he did, and as perky as Francesca. If I stopped talking, though, Dad would jump in again, so I started describing the wild foods and medicinal plants projects, and my invasive plants experiment so far, and the work I'd sent Dimitri, and Mr. Horton, and, not looking at Mom, how vastly more interesting it was than downloaded lesson plans. It was all true too. I was done with lying.

Preston listened. Unlike Dad, who kept interrupting with this obnoxious new term, "loosey-goosey," he listened, nodding, and stirring his espresso with the little spoon, till Milo said, "It's stirred Dad. You're supposed to drink your coffee, not row it."

I was so tense, a laugh escaped.

Milo looked at me gratefully.

Preston, thank goodness, seemed not to have noticed. "Those sound like extremely worthwhile projects," he said. "And, all due respect, Joe, they don't sound particularly loosey-goosey. And, you know, it might be called home-schooling, but the fact is, most parents of teens have neither the time nor the expertise to take on their kids' education." He looked over at Mom. "I wouldn't say it's necessarily the best thing for them either. Adolescence, as we know, is a time for separation."

Milo rolled his eyes at me. I gave him a *No, this is good!* look. They needed to hear this.

"Also, like you," Preston was saying, "most parents I've known tend to start out with a 'school at home' model. But in my experience, most don't stick with it."

"But they do stick with the homeschooling, right?" I put in quickly.

"Oh, absolutely," he said as Milo's eyes rolled up into his head again. "You might not know this, Donna, but the average homeschooling family changes their style of home-schooling seven times in the first two years. So I wouldn't feel bad about not knowing what you're doing."

That was the exact wrong thing to say to her. She looked like she might be starting to hate him.

"He's just saying it's hard to know, Mom," I said. "You have to figure it out as you go along. Right, Preston?"

"That's exactly right," he said. "Because there are as many methods and philosophies of homeschooling as there are families. You do whatever works best, for your beliefs and your life. What my wife and I've settled on over the years is an eclectic, mix-and-match approach. Intellectually rigorous but flexible, interest-oriented but not quote-unquote loosey-goosey . . ."

Milo looked like he was trying not to barf in his latte. But Mom and Dad, I was relieved to see, were nodding now. Though I couldn't tell if that meant they were listening, or just waiting for him to be done, like Milo. Mom was being uncharacteristically silent.

I, however, was starting to almost like Preston. And I loved what he was saying. Especially when he ended: "So if you do decide to give homeschooling another shot, there are plenty of ways to give your kids freedom without being loosey-goosey."

This time it was Milo who let out a laugh, a loud, snorting one. "Sorry," he said. "It's just, you know how when you hear a word enough times it gets funny? Like *noodle*? Or *poodle*. Or *Labradoodle*."

Mom took a quick sip of her cappuccino to cover her smile.

He quickly threw me another *Sorry!* "So . . . you were talking about"—he raised his eyebrow—"quote-unquote freedom, Dad?"

"I was." Preston gave him a quick, disapproving frown, then turned his attention back to Mom and Dad. "I've seen it over and over with kids when they leave school. Some need to veg out for a while to clear their heads, which is fine, I might add, but others, like your daughter, hit the ground running. You can practically see their imaginations catching fire. And if that means she's all over the map, Joe, well, maybe you should give that imagination of hers free rein for a while, let it run free, so to speak, and see where it takes her."

"Exactly!" I nodded. "It's exactly what I've been saying!"

"We've been trying," Mom said.

"That's what started all this," Dad said. "When she read about Wilderness Discovery Camp—"

"Great place!" Preston said.

"It was!" I said.

"Well, she applied without telling us and got herself a scholarship," Dad said. "And we let her go."

"For which I applaud you," Preston said.

Milo was looking so pent-up again, I wondered if he'd now break into applause. But he met my eyes, nodded, and said, "Totally."

Preston smiled at Mom and Dad. "You've obviously got an extremely resourceful, creative daughter."

No wonder I almost liked him!

"Yes, but life isn't summer camp," Dad said. "And summer camp isn't education. And if Kaity really wants to pursue science—"

"Then there are all sorts of great options open to her," Preston said. "From simply finding a better school with a stronger science program, to—if you do decide to keep homeschooling—online science courses on every topic imaginable, weekend ecology workshops, courses over at the community college, outdoor education projects—"

"You hear that, Dad?" My mind was racing. "And you'll help us find them, Preston?"

He nodded. "Oh, absolutely. There's also our homeschool group, which is pretty dynamic. We have a few poets, some actors, a graphic novelist, and, obviously, a musician, but no naturalists. You could present at our group's next *Interest Day*. If you'd like, my wife can even set up a field trip with you for the younger kids. And Donna, we have a mother-daughter book group you might like."

"Mom loves reading," I said. "Don't you, Mom? And she's always saying she needs to read more, right, Dad?" I looked from one to the other, then back at Preston, ignoring Milo's frown. "This sounds fantastic, Preston. It sounds so perfect."

"Whoa!" Dad's hand went up. "Slow down there, Kaity. We're kind of getting ahead of ourselves. Preston, when you were talking about other schools before, did you mean public schools? Because we can't really afford private, but if you think we really could find something good for her, that she likes . . ."

"Chloe loves MVB," Milo said mildly. Too mildly.

What was he doing? I threw him a *This would be a good time to keep your mouth shut* look. But Dad was already going, "Excuse me. Preston, I thought you said you were homeschooling her."

"Not anymore," Milo said.

197

"Why?" Mom said.

"Because she hated being home?" Milo said.

"As I say," Preston said quickly. "One size does not fit all. Things change, needs change, you flex—"

"So then you must think MVB is a decent school," Dad said.

"It's fine," Milo said.

"Not for me!" I said.

Dad put a hand on my shoulder. "Yes, honey, but until we can find you someplace else—"

"Actually, I'm not sure you can for this year, Joe," Preston said. "Plus, I'm not sure you want to start her at a new middle school for just one year. On the other hand, no matter what you decide for high school, if you let her take this year, you'll be giving her a gift she'll remember her whole life." He looked first at them and then at me. "The gift of a year of freedom."

I hadn't realized I'd been holding my breath while they went back and forth. My heart welled up. "Exactly!"

But before I could say another word, or tell what Mom and Dad were thinking, Milo jumped to his feet. "You mean like the freedom I have, Dad?" His voice trembled. "The freedom to sit in my room by myself every morning, talking to nobody, and then at twelve, eat a sandwich with not even Chloe anymore, just you, and then spend the rest of the day in my room practicing . . ." His eyes blazed as he reached down and picked up his violin case and slid out of the booth.

A muscle twitched in Preston's cheek. "That's not actually what his life is like," he said. "He's overstating it a little."

"Right. I forgot." Milo held the case against his chest like a shield. "I get to go to your dynamic homeschool group events. I get to go on your exciting field trips and hang out with the homeschool dorks. I get to teach the little kids theory and violin, and pull crap out of the river, and bag up trash from the side of the road. I get to have my very own yoga mat, and listen to shitty poems, and hear some kid talk about beekeeping. What?" He glared at me like I'd gone over to the Dark Side. "That sounds good to you?"

I looked back at him. *Yes, it does! But I'm not in Preston's clutches. Don't worry! I'm on your side!* I couldn't say it out loud, but he had to see it.

"Fine!" he said. "I have the perfect solution, then. We'll trade places. I'll go to school. You can be me."

He stood there, glaring at all of us, till Mom, looking like she knew full well it was a stupid question, but couldn't stand the silence, said, "So are you saying you're not happy being homeschooled, Milo?"

And Preston, his voice tight as his face, said, "We have this discussion periodically. He has a very demanding schedule. He sometimes chafes at the pressure, but then—"

And Mom, to my amazement, said, "I was asking Milo, Preston. I mean, if we came here to learn what it's really like to be homeschooled—"

"Exactly," Milo said. "You keep saying how one size

doesn't fit all, Dad, and honoring your kid's unique needs and wishes, but when it comes to me—"

"Because you're different, son," Preston said. "You're a very special case."

Milo's chin lifted. "Yeah, well, maybe I don't want to be that special. Maybe I want to be normal, at least some of the time."

"Are you saying you don't want to want to be a musician?" Preston said. "Are you saying you want to give up the violin?"

"No!" Milo's voice rose. "Why do you always say that, Dad? No! But if you make me miserable enough, I might have to."

I felt like my whole side of the table had stopped breathing. I felt like we should put our hands over our ears. Or leave. He stood there, snapping the catch on the violin case open and closed, biting his lip, blinking. My throat ached seeing it.

"Can we talk about this later, son?" Preston said after what felt like forever. "We came here to help Joe and Donna decide about Kaity."

"Katya," Milo shot back. "They might slip up and forget sometimes, but at least they're trying, Dad. They get it. They get that Katya's the person she needs to be. And I need to be Mike."

"What?" His explosion hadn't totally surprised me, but that did.

"Mike?" Preston looked baffled. "What are you talking about? Mike? Why Mike?"

"Because for every kid named Milo there are eight zil-lion Mikes. Mike is a regular person. Mike goes out for wrestling. Or football if he feels like. Mike rock climbs. Mike takes driver's ed. Mike—"

"There's no reason you can't take driver's ed if you want, son." Preston's cheek was twitching again. "But you have to understand. You were blessed with a gift."

"I know that, Dad! But can't I have a life too? I'm not even saying I necessarily want to do those things. I just want to . . ."

"Have a choice," Mom finished for him.

"Like me," I said. No one was listening.

"Go back to deciding Katya's fate," Milo said stiffly. "I'm taking a walk."

"No, Milo, wait!" I said. The last thing I wanted was to leave now, but I couldn't let him go off alone. "I'll come with you."

"You're busy," he snapped, turning to go.

"No, it's fine!" I started to stand.

Mom touched my arm to stop me. "Milo, honey, stay," she said. "Talk to your dad. We can talk to him another time."

"What other time?" I said. "There is no other time!" Milo was halfway across the room already. Preston was up out of the booth, clearly trying to decide whether to follow. "It's Sunday, Mom. Tomorrow's Monday!"

The door banged. Milo was gone.

And now Dad was up too, taking out his wallet. "We'll

take care of the check, Pres," he said. "Go do what you need to do."

"We've all been there, Preston, believe me." Mom picked up her purse. "And we really appreciate your taking the time to—"

"What about trading places?" My voice sounded shrill and desperate. "I mean, not literally. I mean, I'm not a violinist, obviously, and Milo does want to play. I mean, look what happened yesterday. But the school part . . ." I looked from Mom to Dad. It was too hard to look at Preston.

"Do you know how many competitions he's won?" Preston's voice was hoarse. "He can have a very big career if he wants. That's the only reason I—"

"It'll work out, Preston," Dad said. "Don't worry. We have two grown sons, and there were plenty of times they weren't speaking to us. And we got through it, but it took a while, and at the time . . . man!" He shook his head. "You want to do the right thing for your kid, but it's hard as hell to know what that is!"

"Not for us!" I said as, with a stiff nod, and a "Thank you for understanding," Preston headed for the door. "It is trading places," I said. "It is. Really. I'm right. I know I am."

Mom sighed and put her arm around me. "Oh, sweetie, it'd be nice if life was so simple. But it doesn't work like that."

"I'm sorry," Dad said. His eyes looked sad and full of

love. "We know how badly you want things to be different. We'll try to remember not to call you Kaity anymore. You can still be Katya. But sweetheart, I'm afraid that when you get right down to it, bottom line, we're school kind of people."

I could hardly bear to tell Francesca when she called. I didn't tell her about Milo.

"Maybe my appendix will rupture," I said. "And I'll join you in the hospital."

"Or maybe there'll be good things about it."

I could hear her trying to balance hopeful with perky. "Like what?"

"Well, for one, think how glad everyone's gonna be to see you."

Maybe. But how would I explain why I was at school again without sounding like I was crawling back in defeat?

I didn't have to explain anything, as it turned out.

"She missed us, that's all," Alyssa told everyone on the bus Monday morning. "I mean, how long can you stay home?"

"Exactly," I said.

Then, after telling me they liked my hair, that Lindsey and Tyler were over, and that I didn't have to worry about seeing Tyler because he was mostly in the dumb classes, they went back to discussing how Nate had punched Jamie at the game over Serena and broken his nose.

It was the same thing when we got to school: "Hey. Wassup?" "Nothing much." "Did you hear Lindsey and Tyler broke up?" "Yes." "So are you guys gonna get together again now that you're back?" "No." It was the same at lunch. No one but me particularly cared why I was back, or what I'd been doing for the past month. Life was school to them. School was life.

The teachers were a little more surprised to see me. But once they'd given me my books and assigned me a desk, it was business as usual for them too.

The scary thing was how quickly I slipped back into it. I still knew how to take notes on the Constitutional Convention, or forces and motion, or nutrition and healthy lifestyles so that the words went from the teacher's mouth to my notebook without passing through my brain. I knew how to spit it all out again for the five-minute quiz at the end of class. And no problem that it was already October and I'd missed a month. I could have read all the textbook chapters I'd missed while Mr. Berg or Mrs. Pezanowski droned through a single page. But who could I say that to without sounding like someone everyone would hate?

📱 ru okay? I texted Milo during language arts.
not exactly. u?
no. ru mad at me?
no. just mad. & tired & i wanted it to work out for you. blah.
blah, I wrote back.

I called Francesca at the hospital as soon as I got home. "I was wrong when I told you I couldn't do it," I said. "I can do it just fine. I just hate it."

"Well, I thought of another good thing about school to cheer you up," she said. "It's better than having a tube shoved down your nose."

"You have a tube down your nose?" She didn't yesterday.

"I have no tubes at all anymore! They just took out the last one!"

"So does that mean you go home now? And go back to school?"

The thought cheered me more than I'd have guessed.

"No," she said. "I still need to get stronger. But pretty soon!"

So I had one thing to look forward to. But everything else felt like it was specially designed to make me pissed.

"So where's that retired science teacher person Westenburg told you was gonna be in the Resource Room?" I asked Mom that night. "It's Morabito again. But hey, he's got his anger management issues managed." I let out a snore and pretended to fall face-first into my mashed potatoes. "And they gave me Stanley for science again." I pinched my nose and went into a nasally whine. "Okay, people, what is the net force if the wheels of the car apply ten newtons, but a parachute applies seven newtons in the other direction?"

"Well, that's important stuff to know," Dad said. "That's interesting stuff."

"And it's good you've got a real science teacher teaching it to you, instead of me," Mom said. "You've been wanting more real science."

"So then why did they stick me with the worst science teacher in the school? Who already decided last year he didn't like me."

"Hey, I can see how you'd be disappointed," Dad said. "Maybe we can . . ."

I'd stopped listening. Just hearing the word *disappointed* made me furious.

The very next day, when Mr. Stanley had one of his famous sneezing fits in class, he told everyone it was goldenrod giving him the hay fever. Even last year, when I was into being dumb, I knew that wasn't true.

I raised my hand. "The goldenrod's finished blooming," I told him. "Plus, goldenrod doesn't cause hay fever. That's an old wives' tale. It's ragweed."

It came out snarkier than I'd planned, but if I'd caught him in a mistake about something I knew about, who knew what else he was teaching us?

"Well, thank you for straightening that out for everyone, Kaitlyn." Mr. Stanley smiled as if he was glad to be corrected, but now he really hated me.

"We're going to have a little fun today, people," he announced the next day. FORCES CAN BE FUN was written on the board. "Instead of our regular Wednesday quiz we're going to . . ."

"Draw colorful cartoons," I whispered to Jessie, sitting

next to me. Last year Mr. Stanley was very big on colorful cartoons.

But it wasn't the cartoons this time. It was his other idea of fun: haikus. Which in most circumstances I would have loved. But you don't go to science class to do haikus.

"Just to remind everyone," he said as he passed out pages. "The first line of a haiku is five syllables. The second line consists of seven. The last line has five again. I'm giving you thirty-four words or concepts. Pick out three and write haikus expressing them." He ignored the groans from the class. "We'll try a practice one together first. Where friction applies a force but doesn't result in acceleration. Think of an example."

I hadn't read the assignment.

what r u doing? I texted Milo.
sci fi. u?
death by haiku

I shoved my phone in the desk as Mr. Stanley approached.

"Kaitlyn, I don't see you writing. Are you having trouble with the haiku format? Five syllables in the first line. Seven in the second. Five in the third."

"Yes, I know."

His voice was especially annoying today. I picked up my pen and started writing.

"Kaitlyn, please read us your haiku," he said a few minutes later.

"Um . . . it's not really anything," I said.

Jessie peeked over my shoulder and let out a laugh.

He stepped closer. "It must be something, or Jessica wouldn't be laughing. I'm sure everyone would like to hear it."

I covered my paper with my arms. "I don't think that's a good idea."

"Fine." He took the sheet from me. "Then I'll read it. 'Mr. Stanley's voice,'" he read dryly. "'Endlessly grating our nerves. Taking us nowhere.'"

The class dissolved in laughter.

"Forces can be fun!" yelled Zach Martino.

"Hey, it expresses the concept," I said.

Stanley clapped for silence. "Change of plans, people. Since you're obviously not mature enough to handle haikus, we're going to write definitions of every concept on the list." Jessie threw me a dirty look. "All thirty-four. Starting now."

"What are you doing here?" Francesca's eyes practically popped out of her head when she opened the door. She looked better than in the hospital but still not good. Her sweatpants bagged around her hips. You could see her collarbones. "How'd you get out?"

I shrugged. Her house was barely five minutes from the school. "I told Stanley I had to go to the bathroom."

"And then you just walked out the door?" She looked amazed, disapproving, and excited all at once. "You can just do that?"

"Apparently. So how are you?"

"Besides bored?" she said as we walked through an apricot-walled living room full of expensive-looking antiques into a gorgeous kitchen with that pink granite with the white blobs in it that reminds me of salami. "My mom's getting all crazed about the work I missed, so I'm trying to do it. But I don't know if it was always so uninteresting, or if my brain's just not working. So I'm making rice pudding. Which I know is really lame . . ." She took a big pot off the counter and handed me a spoon. "What do you think?" She watched expectantly while I took a taste.

It was wet and gummy and chalky. Also bland.

"Well," I said. "It's sweet."

"I don't get it," she said. "It's so yummy when Gram makes it. Should we throw it away?"

She looked so sad that I said, "No, it just needs things in it."

"What kind of things? And don't say raisins. I hate raisins."

"Chocolate things," I said.

"Let's look!" She dragged a bar stool over to the counter, climbed up, and peered into the top shelf. "My mom hides the goodies up top so I won't, like, scarf them all down. Oh, wow! She didn't tell me she already bought stuff for Halloween." She handed down a box of Oreos, bags of M&M'S and Hershey's Nuggets, and candy corn. "We can mix them in like you do with ice cream!" As she jumped down, she winced and clutched her stomach.

"It still hurts?" I asked.

She shrugged. "Only when I jump. I'm really fine."

"Really? So does that mean you'll be in school soon?"

"I guess." She didn't look too enthusiastic.

"I thought you couldn't wait. You've changed your mind?"

"I don't know." She bit open the bag of M&M'S and poured some out onto the counter. "It's like . . . I know this is gonna sound weird and stupid . . . since I got sick it's like, I'm not an M 'n' M anymore. I'm just an M. Do you know what I'm saying? It's like something's happened to my shell. And I don't know if that's good or bad."

I looked over at her. "Good," I said. "I like you better not all crispy and shiny."

"You do?" Her face unfurrowed a little. "Seriously?"

I nodded.

She began breaking up Oreos. We went back over to the stove and scattered them in the pot, along with handfuls of candy. The candy corn was starting to bleed orange trails into the rice pudding, but otherwise it was looking a lot more appetizing. "Don't you feel like we're, like, nine?" she said as we picked the candy corn out again.

I ate the pieces we'd fished out. "Do I look like I care?"

She brought the bags of candy over to the kitchen island and we sat. "So what made you cut?"

I told her about Mr. Stanley. Her hand went to her mouth as I recited the haiku.

"Uh-oh!" She grimaced when I told about the thirty-four definitions.

"Exactly. And then, of course, everyone's groaning and cursing and yelling out more stupid haikus, so Stanley says that on top of the definitions, we have to write an essay. So now everyone except Zach Martino's totally mad at me." I poured out another heap of M&M'S for us. "And Jessie was already starting to get mad, because yesterday Dylan Davis tried to cheat off my algebra quiz." Which, amazingly, thanks to Cookie, I was actually doing fine with, even though I hadn't done the homework. "And she's madly in love with Dylan. And, I mean, last year I would have pretended not to notice, but it just really irked me, so I turned around and said, 'Hey! Do your own work.' And Ms. Whitehead heard. So then Dylan got a zero. So after class, Jessie's like, 'You know, Kaity, you used to be fun and funny, but you're turning into a real pain in the butt!'"

"Oh, wow. She said that?"

"And at lunch she sat with Lindsey, who she's supposed to hate. And was really cold on the bus."

"Well, I'll sit with you when I get back," she said.

"Seriously?" I thought about her thousands of other friends.

She nodded. "You know, Dylan always cheats. His parents pay him to get A's."

"For real?" I said. "That's disgusting."

"Yeah, well . . . so do mine."

"How much?"

"A lot. It's so I can get into Harvard."

"Yeah, but you don't cheat."

"Well . . ." She made a sheepish face. "Not lately."

"You're kidding!" My mind boggled at the thought of Francesca cheating. "Do you even want to go to Harvard? I mean, this is eighth grade."

"I know. I don't know. I don't know anything anymore. I mean, part of me just wants to be well enough to go back to school, and—"

"Oh, now you want to go back? A few minutes ago—"

"I know. Oh, no! Katya!" She'd gone over to the stove and was looking in the pot. "It's seized up like cement! I can hardly get the spoon out! My mom is gonna kill me!" She looked at the clock. "Uh-oh! And you have to go! If you leave right now, you can probably sneak into the lunchroom. Or . . . oh, wow!" A mischievous look came over her as she noticed I wasn't moving. "We could slice it and put it in bags and hand it out for Halloween."

"Ooh!" I said. "That's disgusting! I love it!"

"I know! See what happens when you cut school and come over here? I start thinking like you! I should join the Homeschool Liberation League!"

I almost choked on a Hershey's Nugget. "Where'd that come from?"

"I don't know." Her face flushed. "Sorry. I know. I can't join. I never homeschooled. I was just thinking . . ."

"That's not why," I said. "There is no Homeschool Liberation League."

"But . . ." She looked even more embarrassed. "But you said . . . Milo said . . ."

"I know. I made it up." I couldn't believe I'd agonized about telling her. "I said it so you'd think I was doing cool, interesting things. I made up a bunch of stuff. Like that—"

"Well, there should be one," she said, as if she hadn't heard, or didn't care. "And I need to be in it. Then, when I do go back, we can—"

"Fine." I went over and pried the rice pudding off the wooden spoon, then touched it to her shoulder. "I hereby dub you an honorary member of the nonexistent, non-homeschool, totally unliberated—"

"I know you don't want to hear this," she said. "I'm probably just being selfish. But I'm gonna be really glad to see you there." She looked at the clock again. "You'd better go so you can get back before the end of lunch. I don't want you to get in any more trouble."

But I didn't much feel like going back to school. So I called Milo.

"I was thinking now might be a good time for another violin lesson," I said after telling him about my morning.

It took him a long time to answer.

"Uh . . . that might not be cool," he said. "But maybe I could come out and meet you later. Can I call you?"

"Yeah, sure," I said.

So I went back to school and somehow made it through the day. But it turned out he couldn't get out later, or the rest of the week. And he had stuff all weekend, even Columbus Day, so I didn't see him then either.

Fiddle360: Blah!

NatureGirl: Blah!

Francesca came back to school Tuesday. And she did sit with me at lunch. And we had some classes together. And that helped.

But instead of trying to figure out what she wanted, and how she felt, the way she'd said when we were at her house, she joined every club and activity she wasn't already a member of, signed up for every committee, and spent a zillion hours on homework.

"I get why you're on the newspaper," I told her after school Thursday. "But Latin Club? Debate team? You hate disagreeing with people. And why would you want to be on Student Council with Dylan Davis?"

"To change things? I don't know."

Friday, she wanted me to go to the newspaper meeting with her. She also wanted me to give Mr. Z. the beaver picture, and go down to the swamp to see how he was doing, and water the planter trays for the garlic mustard experiment.

"Why?" I said. "So you can write about all of it in your article?"

"No!" She swatted me. "So you can stop walking around like your dog died. You're here, okay. So you might as well try to find the good things there are here, and make the—"

"Well, you don't have to worry about your shiny, candy-coated shell," I said. "It's back."

215

Fri Oct 13
I can't believe what a jerk I am.
They're making me go to the counselor
Monday.

SAT 9 a.m.
Just woke Milo up. Told him it was a violin
lesson emergency.

CHAPTER 25

I could hear him practicing before Preston opened the front door—something flashy, lush, and gorgeous, and so good, you'd think it was a CD.

"He sounds incredible!" I told Preston as I followed him to the stairs. It seemed like two months, not two weeks, since I'd been here. I could feel my spirits rising.

"The Mendelssohn concerto," Preston said just as it morphed into something totally not classical. "'War, children . . .'" Milo sang in a raw, rasping voice as the violin wailed out chords—violin as electric guitar, Milo as Mick Jagger. "'. . . it's just a shot away, it's just a—'" He jumped as Preston opened the bedroom door.

My heart skittered, seeing his room again, remembering the last violin lesson. Even with Preston watching, my smile was out of control.

"Hey," I said.

"Hey." It felt like he was trying to scowl at his dad and smile at me, both. Which, for some reason, made him look really sexy. Or maybe it was the scruffy stubble on his chin, or his torn tee and ripped jeans and bare feet, and that

217

smile-but-not-smile, do-not-mess-with-me warning in his eyes. Or the, like, waves of energy coming off him.

"I didn't know you sang," I said.

"That didn't sound like Mendelssohn," Preston said.

"I was just taking a little break," Milo said. "To clear my head."

"A break?" Preston raised his eyebrow. "You just started practicing five minutes ago."

I could see Milo's jaw tense. "Ten, actually."

"Eight weeks, Milo," Preston said. "That's not a long time to get ready. I'm not nagging you. I'm just reminding."

"Reminding counts as nagging, Preston."

Preston nodded. "Point taken. You take mine too, I hope. Enjoy your lesson, Katya."

"You call him Preston now?" I asked as soon as his dad left and shut the door.

Milo snorted. "He said adolescence is a time for separating. So I'm separating. You see now why I haven't wanted you to come over here."

The wild energy was gone. Never mind touching me; he barely looked at me.

I sat on the edge of his desk. "What are you getting ready for?"

He loosened his bow and put the violin back in its case. "A competition."

Even his voice had gone flat.

"So that's what all this pressure is about?"

He nodded.

218

"Competition as in contest? For what?"

He shrugged. "To play the Mendelssohn concerto. With an orchestra in Canada next spring."

"In a big concert hall? In front of a whole audience?"

He nodded again.

I thought of the picture of him I'd printed off the Internet. "And you'd, like wear a tuxedo?" He looked so beautiful in that picture.

"I have one," he said. "But I don't, usually."

"Usually? You've won these things before?"

"Yup."

"So, then, this is like *American Idol*!" I said. "And I get to have you as my violin teacher! So what will you wear? If you win, I mean. Which I know you will."

He stretched a rubber band around a pencil and shot it across the room. "Not if I don't go."

"Excuse me?" I was already picturing myself up there in Canada with him, watching from the first row, clapping till my hands stung.

"I mean, think about it. Eight more weeks of being hounded to practice, and then eight hours in the car with him, each way, to get to the auditions? And then have to sleep in the same hotel room . . ." He shot off another rubber band.

I stood up and took the pencil from him. "Wait a minute. So then you don't get to go, or win, and Preston's even more pissed, and things are even worse?" I thought about Dad telling me that letting my plants die was cutting off my nose to spite my face, and Francesca saying basically the same thing. But Milo looked like he'd cut off my nose if I suggested that. "Listen," I said. "I don't mean to be, like"—I put on a smarmy voice—"'just tell him how you *feeeeeel.*' I'm just saying, I don't think you should miss this, Milo. I think you should talk to him again. Or talk to your mom."

"So she can say, 'Yes, but your father feels really strongly,' and he can give in on a few more things neither one of us gives a crap about? Great news, son!" he said in a perfect imitation of his dad. "I called the high school and found out they'll let you take driver's ed! Once you're sixteen, of course. And you'll be pleased to hear I got you out of the January homeschool confer—"

"Yes, but that sounds like he's trying, at least," I said. "It means he heard you that other time."

"Right." He put on Preston's voice again. "I hear you, son. I hear what you're saying. I feel your pain. I—"

With the heel of his hand, he socked himself in the head.

"Hey!" I grabbed his wrist. "What are you doing?"

"Shutting myself up!" he said. "I mean, here you are, for the first time in weeks, I'm supposed to be your teacher, and what do I do? Whine! About my stupid dad!" He put on a prissy voice: "Ten minutes, actually, Preston." He let out a long hiss of air. "I can't believe I said that! Agggh!" He gave himself another whack with the other hand. "And there I go again! I gotta find some way out of here!"

"Cut it out!" I grabbed that arm too and stood there staring back into his eyes. "You're right. We need to get you out of—"

His eyes suddenly softened. And then his face was coming close and he was leaning toward me, pushing my arms back, pressing me against the wall, kissing me till the stubble on his chin ground into my skin, and my ears were floating, and my lips burned, and I could barely breathe.

Tyler had kissed me tons of times. It wasn't like this.

I let his wrists drop and turned away till the zinging, pinging feeling slowed. When I looked back he was smiling.

"So . . . want a violin lesson now?" he said, looking totally shy suddenly.

Which was fine, because I was feeling really shy too.

He touched my stinging chin. "And maybe I should shave."

"That'd be good," I said.

26

I floated through that night, and all of Sunday.

Then it was Monday. Mrs. Pezanowski said something not true about diabetes in Healthy Lifestyles class, and didn't appreciate when I corrected her. Jessie told me to give it a rest and get over myself. Francesca told Mr. Z. about the beaver. He stopped me in the hall to say he couldn't understand why I didn't think it would make a great story. I didn't totally understand either. Except that I didn't want to be reminded. Then it was time for the counselor.

His office was behind Westenburg's, in what looked like the supply closet. I'd been picturing a pot-bellied, old, short guy with a goatee. Dr. Gordon was young and extremely tall, with a red-and-white-checked shirt, black knit tie, and jeans. With his chair turned so we were facing each other, there was barely room for his legs.

"So, you've been here for two weeks now," he said. "How's it going?"

I moved my chair back as far as I could. "Okay," I said.

"How're your classes?"

"Okay, I guess."

I'd have looked out the window if there was one. There was nothing to see here besides him and a Garfield calendar.

"I hear you haven't been going to all of them," he said. "And that you've been having some difficulty with your teachers."

Here we go, I thought.

"Only because . . ." He seemed too old to get it and too young to know anything. He didn't look that much older than my brother Tommy. "Is that your calendar?"

"No. Why?" He looked at me curiously.

"Just checking. Maybe it's Ms. Pinchbeck's."

I saw a hint of a smile. "Could well be."

"And you're a school psychologist?"

Another smile. "A psychologist," he said. "Who sometimes works in schools. You were starting to say something about your teachers, Katya. You prefer to be called Katya, right?"

I shrugged. "Doesn't matter."

"How come?"

I shrugged again. "Because I don't feel like Katya here."

"What do you feel like here?"

I shrugged again. "I don't know."

I noticed he had an earring hole in his left ear. How long, I wondered, till he'd turn his head so I could see if he had one in the other ear too.

"I had this dream, okay?" I said when he didn't say anything. "And it died. That's how I feel." I didn't like how he was looking at me. "And now you're gonna say, Yes, well, instead of moping around feeling sorry for yourself, making yourself and everyone else miserable, you—"

"No," he said. "I was going to say that doesn't sound too good. You must be really disappointed."

I started to get mad. Then I felt a sudden horrible thickening in my throat. "Yup," I said.

"So what do you think we can do about it, Katya, realistically speaking? Assuming you'd like to try to find something to do about it."

"Like what?" I said. "I mean, it's like the jail warden giving the prisoners better food, right? The food's better, but they're still in jail."

And now there was that faint smile again. "That good, huh?"

"Why are you smiling?"

"Because I remember saying pretty much the same thing to the school shrink. Except you said it better."

"And then what happened?" I asked. "You sucked it up and adapted and got used to it and everything was fine?"

"Actually," he said, "I drove everyone nuts till we found me another school."

"I don't want to go to another school," I said.

I knew I was being a jerk, but it was that or start getting hopes about this guy.

"I wasn't suggesting it," he said. "I was speaking about me." He adjusted his legs. "Not too spacious in here, is it?"

I looked at him. "So when you were driving everyone nuts, were you pissing everyone off too?"

He nodded. "Big-time."

He had no instant answers for me, but I did tell him a little about myself and what was going on, and agreed that turning my friends and teachers against me wasn't all that useful, and said I'd come back next week.

Then I apologized to Francesca. And if I didn't totally lighten up or get over myself, I managed not to actively piss anyone off for the next few days. So it almost killed me when Milo texted me in science:

dunno if you can get out now, but it's pretty bad around here.

what's going on? I replied.

just more of the same. blah.

O, I WISH I COULD, I wrote back.

I was dawdling in the hall with Francesca on my way to the Resource Room when Mr. Kelly, the music teacher, waved to me.

"Hey! We've missed you in marching band this year," he called.

"I've switched to violin," I called back.

"Really." He stopped walking. "That's the best news I've heard all day!"

When he smiled, Mr. Kelly looked more like a kid than a teacher. I smiled back at him.

"I didn't know I was *that* bad."

"I just meant, I'm desperate for violins in the high school

orchestra," he said. "I conduct that too, you know. I don't get why no one wants to play violin these days. I've got a really strong cello section, winds and brass up the kazoo . . ."

"I'm hoping I won't have to be at MVB next year," I said.

"What?" Francesca looked startled. I hadn't told her or anyone about my talk with Dr. Gordon. "Where are you going?"

I shrugged. "No clue. Just not here."

"Then join now," Mr. Kelly said. "I'll take an eighth grader. Hey, I'll take a third grader if she plays violin."

I made a face. "I've only had, like, two lessons."

"Yes, but by December, you'll have had . . ."—he counted on his fingers—"ten, which means I can put you in the second violin section in the winter concert. You think I'm joking? We're talking desperation here, ladies. If you can hold a violin, read music, and count, I can use you."

"You should do it," Francesca said. "Maybe I should too. Think Milo wants another violin student?"

"I don't know, but . . ." I might have no clue for myself, but I suddenly saw exactly how to help Milo! "Mr. Kelly!" I said. "What if you had a really good violinist? I mean, a prize-winning violin prodigy? Because my . . ." Should I say boyfriend? I was aching to say that out loud to someone, but was this the time? ". . . friend Milo Mathias, who's also my violin teacher—"

"Milo Mathias?" Mr. Kelly's eyes sharpened. "Seriously? I heard him play at the Unitarian Society last year. Oh, man,

I would love to get him for the orchestra. He's thinking of coming to MVB next year?"

"He'd come right now," I said. "If he can talk his father into it."

"Or if Katya can," Francesca said.

"Well, talk fast!" Mr. Kelly said. "Because my concert master just dropped orchestra for soccer, and winter concert is fast approaching. The concert master's the guy who leads the violin section," he told Francesca, as if any friend of Milo's would obviously know. "And I'm thinking if Milo's already got teaching experience, he might be able to help out with coaching, because I'm not a string player."

"Would you talk to him, then?" My heart raced as if this was the answer to my problem, not Milo's. "I mean, Milo's father."

"Gladly," he said. "Have him give me a call."

I blew off Resource Room once again and called Milo.

"I know how to get you into school!" I said.

"Put out a hit on my dad?" he said.

"No! Get him to talk to our music teacher!" I quickly told him what Mr. Kelly had said. "And you know how Westenburg, who's like a thousand times more rigid than your dad, couldn't wait to make quote *special arrangements* so my parents would send me back here, because I'm so quote *gifted and talented*? Well, if he'd do that for me, Kelly can get the high school to do it for you, who's mega-gifted and super talented." I was so eager to get the words out, I was getting tangled. "Or maybe you should talk to Kelly first, before you talk to your dad. Or I could do it with you. We could go this afternoon, after school. I can set it up right now. What do you think?"

He took so long to answer, I checked to make sure I hadn't lost the call.

"Hello?" I said. "You're not saying anything. Is everything okay?"

"Yeah. Fine," he said. "We had another fight just now, that's all."

"But you think it's a good idea, right?"

"I think it's a great idea," he said. "And I think you're . . . really . . ."

"Then why don't you sound happy?" I said.

"Because I still don't see him saying yes," he said.

When he turned up at my door with his violin the next day, about two minutes after I got off the bus, I was sure it was with good news. He'd never been to my house before.

One look at his face killed that idea.

"Got a Frisbee?" was all he said. So we went out and threw it around and then, still not talking, wandered in the woods till dinner. He stayed for dinner. Then, after helping clean up, we went into the den, and, with Waffle sitting on his foot the whole time, and me attempting to do homework—Dr. Gordon had convinced me that not doing it didn't really help—Milo practiced for three hours.

Now we were sitting on the floor, carefully not touching—Mom and Dad were in the next room, watching the ten o'clock news—but as close as you could be and not.

"Is there seriously a fish called 'fluke'?" he asked. I'd been staring at the same page of my English text for the past ten minutes while he riffled through Mom's cooking magazines. "And would you really want it with zippy mango salsa?"

"Not a lot," I said.

He lifted a strand of my hair and curled it around his finger. "How 'bout with creamy, healthy slaw?"

"I don't think so."

"Or oven-toasted macadamias?"

"No! Stop!" I snatched the magazine and bopped him with it, then dropped the English textbook in his lap. "Here. If you want to read something, read me this!"

It was the longest time we'd ever spent together. Jess and Alyssa were always saying you couldn't have a romantic thing with a boy and be friends with him both. They were so wrong.

"I see you shaved," I said.

"Yep." He slid closer, so that the whole length of his leg pressed against mine. I was sure he was going to kiss me. "You'd rather hear 'The Fall of the House of Usher' than 'Flaky, Fantastic Fluke'?"

I punched him. "Would you stop with the fluke? *You're* a fluke!"

"Hey!" He grabbed me. "That's my bow arm! Cut it out!"

"What? I barely touched you!"

I didn't hear the doorbell ring. It must have, though, because Waffle ran to the den door, barking. Then the TV went off and I heard Dad's voice, from the living room, saying, "Oh, hello, Preston. You here to pick up Milo?"

We had the door closed, thank goodness, but even so, Milo flinched and moved away from me. I scrambled to my feet and grabbed Waffle's collar. He quit barking just in time for me to hear Preston say the words *cool down* and thank them for giving Milo dinner. "I presume he ate with you?" he said.

"Oh, yes," Mom said. "It was really fun. He's great company."

"And very funny," I heard Dad say. "He cracked us up with his imitations."

"Of me, I take it?" Preston said.

I'd moved up to the door to hear better. Milo came over alongside me. I took his hand. I could almost feel the waves of tension coming off him.

"No, no!" Mom assured Preston. "Just some of the characters he's met at his auditions. I have to tell you, Preston, you said he was talented, but I didn't know he was that good!"

Milo cursed under his breath. "Don't get him started!"

Preston's voice had warmed. "He played for you?"

"No," Mom said. "He was just practicing."

"He was practicing?" Preston sounded amazed.

"Yeah. Till just a little while ago," Mom said.

"Well, maybe my wife was right, then," Preston said. "She said I should let him stay out, and not call."

"Duh!" Milo muttered.

"And how've you all been doing?" Preston was saying. "Better than us, I hope."

"Oh, we're okay," Dad said. "Kaity's been having some adjustment pains, but I guess that's to be expected."

This time the one going "Duh!" was me.

"Well, guess we should tell him I'm here." Preston didn't sound too happy. "A woman who's considering loaning him a very valuable old violin is in town, and we're supposed to be playing for her first thing tomorrow morning. It's a Tononi." He said it as if everyone would recognize the name. "I'm just hoping he agrees to go. I can't say I've got the stomach for another battle."

Milo groaned.

"Why does there have to be a battle?" Mom said. "I mean, this sounds like a great opportunity for him. He doesn't want it?"

Milo gripped my fingers.

"He doesn't want anything I want at the moment," Preston said. "At the moment all he wants is to get out of the house and go to school."

And this is news? I felt like shouting. *You really had to come here and tell us this and ruin our perfect day?* If the den had a back door I'd have smuggled Milo out and hidden him in the tree house.

But then Dad said, "Listen, Pres. Feel free to tell me to shut up, because it's not my business. And I don't pretend to know anything about the music world, but you know, if he's really that unhappy . . . I mean, I know his sister's at school . . ."

"What are you saying, Joe?" Preston's voice sounded strained. "Are you saying I should just give up and let him go to school?"

I stopped breathing.

"Maybe," Dad said. "I mean, if he wants it that much."

Silence.

Milo gripped my hand harder.

"You sound like my wife," Preston said finally.

"Well, then," Mom said. "Not that it's my business either. But maybe you should be listening?"

"I'm just afraid we'll be starting down a slippery slope." Preston's voice was even tighter. "This is a crucial point in his career, not to mention his lessons in New Haven twice a week, and his rehearsals. I don't see how that can possibly fit in with school—"

"Yes it can!" I cried, opening the door and stepping through to the living room. Preston, still in his coat, and looking even more upset than that time in New Haven, stood halfway between the couch and the front door, holding a down jacket. "I've been talking to Mr. Kelly," I said. "The music teacher. He knows who Milo is. He said he'll do anything to get Milo at the high school so he can be in his orchestra. Did Milo tell you?" I looked at Milo, who'd come over beside me. He was biting his lip, as if he didn't trust himself to talk.

Preston adjusted his glasses on his nose. "No. He didn't. But his mother mentioned it."

232

"Well, did she tell you everything I found out?" I went on. "About how the high school makes flexible arrangements all the time for kids who are on, like, work study, job shadowing, assignment things? And that Mr. Kelly was sure something like that can be worked out for Milo too?" Milo was nodding now. "I mean, you'll have to talk to Dr. Sherman, the high school principal, but . . ." I told him everything I knew for sure, and some things Francesca had found out for me, and some things I just hoped and prayed were right. "So you won't be giving up anything," I said. "Except the battles."

The muscle in Preston's cheek twitched. Had I gone too far? No. Mom and Dad were nodding too.

"Well, Katya," Preston said, taking off the glasses now. His face looked weirdly naked. "I have to say, you've certainly done your homework. And Milo, you certainly do have an advocate here."

"Yes, well," Dad said. "As you pointed out, she's pretty creative and resourceful."

"Yeah, Dad!" Milo said. "If you won't listen to me, listen to her."

"Forget me!" I said. "Doesn't that sound like it could work, Preston?"

Mom threw me a warning look. "She's also a little pushy."

"It's okay, Donna," Preston said. "I'd say my son's lucky to have her for a friend."

"So then are you going to look into it?" I said. "Because if you need people's names and numbers at the school . . ."

Mom was the first one to laugh. But then Dad started laughing. Even Preston's face began to relax.

"Why don't you go ahead and e-mail them to me, Katya?" he said. "And Milo and I can talk with his mother when we get home." He handed Milo the jacket he'd been holding. "Here, put your jacket on, son. It's very cold."

"I don't need . . ." Milo started, but then he took it and looked at me with eyes so full of hope and joy and thanks, I almost burst. "Yeah, okay, Dad," he said.

27

He sounded about to bubble over when he called the next night.

"It worked! We did it! I'm outta here! He made me sign this ridiculous, like, contract, with this, like, whole practicing schedule attached, and these Not Mike clauses where I agree not to do anything that would injure my precious hands, and it won't happen till after the competition, but I don't care! I'm free!"

"Yay! That is so good, Milo! I'm so happy!" I closed my English book. I was still trying to read that story for the quiz tomorrow.

"Oh, and I am gonna get the Tononi, by the way. We worked it out with the lady this morning!"

"So your dad must be happy too," I said.

"I think he is. It's kind of amazing. The only bad thing so far"—his voice turned hesitant—"I won't be able to hang out that much till after the competition. From now till December sixteenth, I'm basically gonna be practicing. I'll go into school for a few orchestra rehearsals, but—"

I felt a flash of worry. "Can we still do my lessons?"

"Oh, yeah!" he said. "We're not giving up your lessons. You can borrow my old violin if you want, once I get the Tononi. Plus, starting in January, I'll be in the high school building, right next door to you. I can see you every day."

"Unless my folks cave too." *Whoa!* Why had it taken me so long to think of that? "I mean, they were the ones who told Preston you should listen to your kids, right?"

As soon as we hung up, I went down to the living room, and after announcing Milo's good news, which they cheered, I said, "We need to talk again about my leaving school."

Dad clicked off the TV and sat up. "You're just starting to get used to it."

"No," I said. "I'm not. What you said about Milo last night, it's true for me too. If I'm really that unhappy, it won't work for anyone."

Mom put down her knitting. "Yes, but there's a difference between you and Milo, honey. You're okay. Milo really isn't. You might not be jumping for joy at school, but—"

"That's right," Dad said. "I mean, face it, kiddo. How many people really like school? It is what it is. And it does what it needs to do for you."

"And just think," Mom said. "With Milo right there, you'll be able to see him every day."

"Yeah, well," I said. "I'd trade it in a heartbreak for being free."

It wasn't till I was halfway to the stairs that I realized the slip I'd made. I don't know if they caught it. If they did, they didn't say anything.

Dr. Gordon looked at me, slumped down in the chair across from him.

"And here I was hoping you had a better week," he said.

"Yeah, doesn't pay to hope, does it?" I told him how Mom and Dad had killed my dream yet again.

"Yes, but other than that, Mrs. Lincoln," he said, "how was the play? How'd everything else go?"

"Nothing great," I said. "Well, actually, one really great thing did happen." I told him about Milo.

He sat back in his chair and folded his arms. "And you made that happen."

Was he asking or telling? "Well, me and my parents."

"Yes, but basically you. I'm impressed."

"Then why can't I make anything happen for me?" I said. Whined. Even I could hear myself whining. Which made me a little embarrassed to look at him. "Those are cool boots," I said after a bit. He had on cowboy boots today.

"Glad you like them," he said.

"You know, I have this friend I think should come see you," I said. "She keeps saying she doesn't want to be the way she is. But it's like, the more she sees through everything at school, and says she doesn't like it, and wants to be different, the more she stays the same. She's really, really smart, and I keep thinking she gets it, but she's like, totally confused . . ."

He nodded. "It's confusing. And complicated. It's good you're talking about it with her. You know, wanting to change is the first step."

I sat up straighter. "So when you changed schools, were you in middle school?"

"Can I read you this?" Francesca asked. I'd been hearing her keyboard click the whole time we'd been on the phone.

"Sure. Why not."

I'd just finished reading to her how High Expectations High expected its students to make interdisciplinary connections through observing and understanding connections within and between disciplines. Instead of doing homework these past two nights, I'd been looking at school websites.

She cleared her throat. "'Want to know what it's like to start school for the first time at the age of eleven? When asked that question, sixth grader Chloe Mathias says, 'It's cool riding the bus with all the kids. I've got a great bunch of teachers.' When asked her favorite subject . . .' Oh, ughhhh! I hate this!" she moaned. "It is so perky and boring!"

"Well, it's better than this." I put on a ringing, high-falutin voice. "'Our school is a kindergarten-through-life community of learners dedicated to meeting individual learning styles to prepare students to meet the demands of today and the—'"

"Didn't you just read me that last night?" she said.

"Noooo. That one said . . ." I clicked to another page I'd bookmarked: "'In an atmosphere of equality, acceptance, and respect, students prepare to contribute to our demo-cratic society and an interdependent world.'"

"They sound like they were written by Westenburg," she said.

"Yeah, it's like they're all the same school, with the exact same pictures of the exact same smiling students."

"It's not really called High Expectations High, though," she said. "You made that up."

"Yes, but I didn't make up the quotes. I swear to God. What about the Chloe quotes? Did she honestly say that?"

I still hadn't gotten to know Chloe. I just knew that she looked like a gawkier, goofier Milo, right down to the raised eyebrow, and that every time I saw her she was wearing the same black outfit, including the black knit hat, pulled down almost to her eyebrows. It was hard to picture Chloe perky.

Francesca snorted. "No, she said there were too many inane rules, the bells make her crazy, and the boys are deeply dorky. But she likes the bus. And lunch. And she loves her locker."

"Cool. So why don't you say that?"

"I know. That would have been interesting at least. But if I write that, someone will just perkify it."

"Then you'll change it back again. You're trying to please them before they've even objected! This is your article and your idea, right? You're done playing the game."

"You're right," she said. "You're totally right. It's just so hard."

"I know," I said. "You need to talk to Dr. Gordon."

"I need the Homeschool Liberation League!"

"The now-defunct former non-homeschool non-liberation league?" I went back into my highfalutin voice. "When asked what it's like to start school for the first time at the age of eleven, Chloe Mathias said, 'I love being part of a passionate community of empowered interdisciplinary disciplinarians. I hope thereby to achieve diversity and biodiversity and go on to Onward and Upward High.'"

"Where I will be individually empowered," Francesca added.

"But perky," I said.

"Kaity," Mom called through the door. "It's late! You've been on for two hours!"

"No, I haven't!" I called back. "Francesca and I are doing homework."

"So are they gonna take you around to look at these places?" Francesca asked.

"Nah, they want me to utilize effective problem-solving strategies to resolve social and emotional issues. In other words, shut up and accept my fate."

"Good," she said. "I mean, not good. I mean, I don't want you to leave. Unless I do."

"What?" My mind jumped to all the fancy, expensive prep schools I'd been looking at. "You're not leaving? Are your parents . . . ?"

"No. I just sometimes . . . I mean, that thing you said about how I still have my candy-coated shell—"

"I know!" I said. "Sorry! That was so horrible! I am so—"

She cut me off. "I know. But I just wonder . . . I mean, if I was in a different place, would it be easier to be, you know . . ."

"Somebody else?"

"Exactly! And I keep wishing, when I do finally finish this Chloe part, that you would write the next part, with all the reasons you don't want to be there—the hypocrisy, and the busywork, and the cheating, and the worrying about all the wrong things, and the sucking up, not to mention spending all year on test prep and—"

I cut her off this time. "I don't want to write about it. There's no point writing about it. I just want to leave. You're the one on the newspaper. Besides, you're the one who just came up with all the reasons."

She sighed into the phone. "I know. I just keep thinking, if we did it together . . ."

"Four . . . four . . . two . . . three . . . three . . . one . . ." To the tune of "Lightly Row" I sang out the name of each finger I placed on the string, while Milo, on his own violin, wove a ridiculously high and crazily complicated accompaniment around me, turning what had to be one of the lamest songs in the universe into something unbelievably gorgeous.

"Whoa! And who said you won't be ready for orchestra?" he said with a proud grin as I somehow made it to the last note.

"Seriously? My part didn't sound too horrible? So you think I can play in the winter concert?"

241

"Seriously?" he said, setting his violin down on his desk. "No." He straightened my bow for the hundredth time and tried to loosen my thumb on the fingerboard. "But you're picking it up fast. And seriously? If we're going to keep doing this, you're gonna need to start practicing."

And when you get the Tononi I can borrow your violin? I started to say. Instead, I heard myself saying, "What are you, Preston?" I intended it as a joke. But even I could hear the edge in my voice. Which I didn't mean. I'd been having a really nice time. And not just because we'd been in his room alone for two hours. I liked learning the violin. Milo was a great teacher. "Sorry," I said. "I'm just really bummed and grouchy."

"I noticed." He didn't look at me as he loosened the bow and put away the violin. "Is it because things are working out for me and not for you?"

"No. No," I said. "I'm happy for you. Really, Milo. I'm really happy. It's just . . ."

This whole week, every time we talked, I'd restrained myself from pissing and moaning. Now it all spilled out, including a repeat of Tuesday's rant to Francesca about school websites.

"So have you looked at New Directions?" he asked.

I groaned. "You mean High Expectations High? Where knowledge meets imagination? Probably. I've looked at every charter, public, alternative, magnet middle, and high school website between Hartford and New Haven." I reached over and pushed back a hunk of hair flopping into

242

his face and did a snip-snip thing with my fingers. "Where are your scissors?"

He ignored me. "And?"

I pulled out my collar and pretended to barf down my shirt. "They're exactly the same. They sound exactly like MVB."

"Which is why you should look at New Directions," he said. "It's this new charter high school over in Baybrook." He seemed excited. "It's part of this new Shoreline Park Environmental Education Project my mom's involved with. She writes their grants for them. It's got an organic farm that the kids all have to work on, where they grow the food for the school, and they do all this ecology, environmental stuff. Which I know sounds kinda Birkenstockian crunchy-granola loosey-goosey. But I was talking to her about you the other day, and she said they do really good science stuff. They look at climate change indicators, and do stream pollution studies, and plant and wildlife inventories, and I can't remember what else, but it's the stuff you like. And it wouldn't get you out of MVB this year, but—"

"Then what good is it?" I said. "Even if it is 'new'?"

"Hey!" He glared at me. "Are you gonna be a total creep about this? Because I was about to invite you to go there with me Saturday."

In spite of myself my heart rose. "Why? Are you thinking of going there?" I had to admit, it sounded interesting.

"No, but they're having some, like, fall-harvest-festival-family-fun-weekend thing this weekend. You know, to get the garden cleaned up for winter."

I looked at him. "That doesn't sound like your kind of fun. Especially not with your family."

"What do you mean? I like raking up rotten tomatoes and shoveling compost and savoring the bounties of the harvest."

"You do not."

"You don't know that. I liked eradicating."

I narrowed my eyes at him. "Your mom's making you go, isn't she? You just need company."

"No!" He scowled back at me. "You really are being a creep today!"

He hooked an arm around my neck and pulled me down onto the beanbag chair with him. We were so wedged in, I couldn't sit up or wiggle away.

"Your dad's gonna come in!" I warned.

"I'll tell him it's a relaxation exercise," he said. "To loosen up your bow arm. And to get you to stop being such a jerk. I'll tell him you needed an attitude adjustment."

"And how are you going to do that?" I challenged.

Next thing I knew, he'd started tickling.

"Do not tickle me!" I yelled. "I hate being tickled! You're wasting your time, Milo! I'm not ticklish!"

"Oh, yeah! I can see that!" He loomed over me with this ridiculously cross-eyed, fiendish expression as I squealed and giggled and kicked my legs around like a three-year-old.

"That is so obnoxious, Milo! Cut it out!" I yelled, laughing even harder.

"Then stop feeling sorry for yourself and come to this stupid family fun thing with me."

It's weird when you've been laughing and/or fighting—I still wasn't sure which—and all of a sudden you stop, and there's this thrumming silence. It felt like after we were kissing, the last time I was here.

"Did you notice I shaved for you?" he said when we finally got up.

I was worried my voice would come out all thick and dazed, so I just smiled.

"So now, are you gonna go with me or not?" he said. "It's this Saturday. And forget the name, okay? I mean, it's not like your name's so cool."

"We won't be able to afford it," I said. "It's gotta be really expensive."

"Hey!" He held up his fist like he was going to punch me. "Are you gonna turn into a creep again? I told you. It's not a private school. It's public. And we don't know yet, but it might be someplace good."

"I know," I said.

It sounded so good to me, I was afraid to hope.

28

"Go without me," Milo said Friday night. He'd called to tell me he and Preston had to pick up the new violin Saturday. "We can probably get over to Baybrook by mid-afternoon. You can hang with my mom and Chloe."

"I don't know your mom," I said, imagining a female version of Preston. "I hardly know Chloe."

"They're nice. You'll get to know them."

"Argh, Milo!"

"Then get your folks to take you," he said. "Go with Francesca or somebody. Are you gonna be a creep again? Just go. You know you're curious."

So there I was, Saturday afternoon, at Shoreline Park, with Mom and Dad. Who, aside from worrying what would happen if the place actually looked good to me and they had to figure out how to get me there, were clearly trying to take their cue from me. Which was hard, because I had no idea.

That's not true. I liked the outdoor part as soon as I saw it: a huge fenced-in vegetable garden guarded by demented-looking scarecrows dressed for Halloween; a pumpkin field full of kids picking out their pumpkins; long rows of rust and gold chrysanthemums and purple asters. Most of the people bustling around with rakes and trash bags looked pretty old. But there were also little kids tossing food to an evil-looking goose, then jumping back, shrieking with laughter, and bigger kids forking leaves into a cart, and a high school kid cranking an old-fashioned cider press while others threw in apples. It looked like camp. It looked great.

The kids seemed kind of okay too, from what I could tell—some cool, some not; some dressed like the kids at camp: torn jeans, flannels, dreads, bandannas; and not all white, like MVB. That was something new and interesting. The school, on the other hand, looked dismal—a long, small-windowed, two-story, mottled brick building that seemed like a warehouse, or a former jail. It was also freezing cold here, with a bitter wind blowing off Long Island Sound. It blew my hair out of its braid instantly.

I was searching the pockets of my fleece for a barrette when a tall Milo-ish-looking woman in muddy jeans and a Windbreaker came to greet us.

"Hi, welcome! I'm Milo's mom, Sandy." She pulled off her work gloves to shake our hands. Milo was right. She seemed nothing like Preston. "And you must be the famous Katya! We're still hoping the sun will come out. Chloe, come on over and say hi to Katya's mom and dad."

Unlike everyone else, in their heavy work clothes, she had on black skinny jeans, a thin black cardigan, black Chinese Mary Janes, and her usual black hat.

"Hey," she said.

"We have hot and cold cider," Sandy said. "And the donuts are homemade."

Chloe nodded. "I've eaten seven."

"No eating till we've done some work!" Dad said. We were all keeping up the fiction that we'd just come for the garden cleanup. "We're all gardeners here."

"Excellent!" Sandy said. "I've heard great things from Preston about all of you. Let's get you some rakes." As she walked us to the tool shed, she pointed out the various garden plots, the chicken coops and goat pen, the cold frames and greenhouse, and root cellar. "The kids do most of the tending," she said. "They take care of the animals too. Everyone has to work on the farm."

Chloe and I trailed behind.

"She'd love it if I went here," Chloe said, wrinkling her nose.

"So do you know anyone who does?" I looked around at the kids again. They seemed really into what they were doing. Or at any rate, not interested in me.

"No, that's why I ate seven donuts," she said. "It was that or rake rotten tomatoes. When they freeze, they like, liquefy and squish down, and then they're, like, hidden under the dead leaves where you can't see them. Please tell me you're not a gardener! I've been waiting all day for you to get here so I'd have an excuse to go inside." She shivered. "If it was up to me, I'd go inside on Columbus Day and come out at Easter."

"Not me," I said, following her toward a side door. "I'd go out and stay out."

"I know," she said as she opened it. "Milo told me not to make any snide remarks about the school. He said you were snide enough already."

I liked Chloe.

There seemed to be no one else in the building. The inside wasn't as dismal as the outside. Instead of green and beige, like MVB, the walls were bright colors. Instead of Westenburg's cheery inspirational sayings, there were giant photos of smiling kids building things or working in the gardens, or standing over pots in a gleaming kitchen.

It still smelled like school, though.

"Do you think there's some kind of air spray or something that schools all buy to keep kids in control?" I said. "Like anti-pheromones? And why does every school have these horrible fluorescents lights? They make you feel like pimples on parade."

"Oh, wow," Chloe said. "You're even more negative than me."

I peered into a classroom. It looked like a classroom.

"Only about school," I said.

"I kind of like it," she said.

"The smell or school?"

"School," she said. "It's kind of nice being told what to do by someone who's not your parents."

"Even if what they're telling you is stupefyingly boring?"

She looked sheepish. "I sort of like my teachers. I don't

actually mind the smell, either. It smells like . . . I don't know . . . like . . . things are gonna happen."

"Bad things," I said.

I had to admit, though, that the posters on the walls here looked kind of interesting: Lots of stuff on climate change and global warming, of course, but also The Politics of Growing Food, The Food Chain, Beneficial Insects. They even had the same Invasive Plants of Connecticut poster Mr. Horton had given me.

I showed Chloe the Asiatic bittersweet. "That's actually what got Milo and me together, would you believe? Eradicating bittersweet. That and garlic mustard."

"Really." A tall, squarish woman with short white hair came up beside me. "Hello, Chloe." She had on a heavy gray turtleneck and work boots.

"Oh, hi Meg," Chloe said. "This is Katya."

"Who is not too fond of school, I gather," Meg said with a slight raise of her eyebrows. "Anti-pheromones. That can't be good."

Chloe stretched her mouth at me like, *Wanna leave?*

"Do you know about our clipping walks, Katya?" Meg said. "Once a month, we take a stretch of the Shoreline bike trail and clear vines. They grow faster than we can clip, but we're trying. You should join us." She had a husky voice and a brisk, bordering on brusque, way of talking. "I've got a handout in my office somewhere. If you come upstairs, I'll see if I can dig it out of the rubble.

"So how did you get interested in non-native species?" she

asked as the three of us headed down the hall to the stairs.

"This old man friend of mine," I said. Uh-oh. Had I insulted her? She wasn't exactly young. "He's old, but he's still really sharp," I said. "He goes out in his truck every day and looks for bittersweet to chop down. He also pulls up spotted knapweed and garlic mustard."

"Excellent!" she said. For an old lady, she was taking the stairs very fast. "We need more people like him. We've been having a wretched time with the garlic mustard here."

"Everywhere," I said. "I know. I hate it."

"Our deer, which decimate everything else, won't touch it," she said.

I nodded. "And you know, it's crowding out all sorts of native plants, and possibly trees."

She stopped and looked at me. "How does it do that?"

She had extremely bright blue eyes with wrinkles around them, and this way of peering at me that was friendly and inquisitive and challenging all at once. And maybe humorous, but maybe not. Which should have been scary, except that for some reason, I wasn't scared.

"It has these chemicals in the roots that, like, kill the good . . ."—*Funguses* sounded too much like athlete's foot, so I went with the way that rhymed with *bungee*—"fungi that other plants and trees need to get their nutrients . . ." Chloe looked at me like, *You're talking about this why?* But Meg was listening, nodding.

"Fun-jeye," she corrected me. "These symbiotic relationships are so interesting. And complicated."

251

"I know," I said, embarrassed by my mistake, but somehow not caring. We were walking down the hall now. "I don't know too much about that side of it. I'm better at just, like, pulling out the plants."

"You'd better keep reading, then," she said.

"Well," I said. "I did actually start a little experiment, to see if garlic mustard plants would stop vegetable seeds from sprouting."

"What did you find?"

"Nothing, actually. I kind of . . . let it drop."

"Why is that?" she said.

Luckily, I was saved from answering as she opened a door into a bright, plant-filled, incredibly messy office. Every surface was covered with books and papers.

"I was supposed to be doing my filing this morning," she said. "But I got distracted with potting up basil plants for the winter. I'm not sure why I bother. They never make it through."

"Whitefly," I said. "That's what always gets my dad's."

"And what does he do for whitefly?"

"I'm not sure," I said. "Maybe ladybugs? Or something. He's not into poison." A thought hit me: "I wonder if garlic mustard could be used as a repellent."

She gave me that maybe humorous, definitely challenging look again. "Something else for you to research." She saw Chloe eyeing the photo behind her desk of two girls with their arms around an enormous, lumpy pumpkin. "You remember Bubba, don't you, Chloe? The kids named it Bubba," she told me. "It grew in the compost last year."

"My dad's a very big compost fan," I said.

She looked at me. "And you?"

"Well, I don't necessarily want to get up close and personal with it, like he does," I said. "I'm not a fan of worms."

Chloe cleared her throat. "On that note, if you guys don't mind, I think I'll find the girls' room. Katya, I'll meet you downstairs, in the library."

"So I'm curious what it is about garlic mustard that intrigues you so," Meg said when Chloe left.

"I don't know," I said. I'd never thought about it. "I guess, just that we ought to be able to do something about it. Or turn it into something useful." Meg was nodding again. "I actually wrote to this plant scientist guy at Yale with this idea I had for trying to control it."

"Really." She went over to her desk and sat down. "What'd he say?"

"He never answered," I said. "But it was a pretty bad idea."

"Or you wrote to the wrong guy," she said. "What department was he in?"

"Plant biology." I was looking at a picture on the back wall of kids in caps and gowns.

"Our first graduating class," she said. "You might do better with someone from an environmental research center. Or you could try the Department of Ecology, Evolution and Environmental Biology, down at Columbia. Unless you've already done that."

"No, but . . ." I told her about my Food Network idea. "I thought maybe if chefs could come up with delicious things to do with it . . ." I made a face. "They didn't answer me either."

She smiled. "Maybe you're just ahead of your time."

Before I knew it I was blurting, "What about using it for school lunches? I was thinking how you guys use the vegetables from the garden for feeding students. What about if you did a combination eradicating/harvesting/utilizing thing?"

Her eyebrows went up slightly. "Have you tasted garlic mustard?"

"I tried a leaf."

"How was it?"

"Kinda bad," I said.

She laughed. "So the deer are right."

"But it might be better cooked. And I read it's better in the spring. Plus, school lunch isn't supposed to be good."

"True enough," she said.

"And you have those pictures on the wall of cooking classes. You could probably come up with some good recipes."

"Or you could," she said.

"Or we could bring your goat on one of the clipping walks. That was actually sort of what I wrote to the plant biology guy."

"So why are you so anti-school, Katya?" she said. She pointed to the chairs. "You know, you can sit."

I took the chair closest to her desk.

"I'm not anti-school," I said. "School's great for some people. I mean, Chloe really likes it. I have friends who like it. Just not me."

I told her about my back and forth year so far, starting with how I felt at camp. I shocked myself by adding: "That's how this feels to me here. Like my camp."

"Well, thank you," she said. "Having taught in many schools for many years, I take that as a major compliment. But it's hardly camp here. Yes, everyone works on the farm, but the curriculum includes all the traditional subjects as well, at the college prep, honors, and AP levels only. Our students work very hard."

"That's okay," I heard myself say.

She was still talking: "Small . . . project based . . . collaborative . . . conservation biology . . . environmental health of local rivers . . . computer spreadsheets . . . strong writing focus . . ."

It sounded so good, I could barely slow my mind enough to listen. "So if I did want to come here, who would I talk to?"

"You're talking to her now," she said. "I'm the dean of students."

My heart jumped. "I thought you were the science teacher."

Her smile widened just a little. "Don't worry. We have a pretty good science teacher."

"So then . . . is there any way you can let me start here now?" I blurted. "I can deal with the worms."

"That's good to know," she said. "But I'm afraid we only take incoming freshmen in the fall. However, we are increasing the size of the freshman class next year. I'll be happy to give you the application packet so you can see what we'll need." She opened a drawer and handed me a stapled sheaf of papers, talking about the communities they drew from, and the mix of kids, how the preliminary application was due in January, about the essay, and the last quarter report card, and how they usually required an interview.

Usually? Was she saying I wouldn't need one?

"And do you ever take homeschoolers?"

She looked at me curiously. "Yes. If they're strong candidates and meet all the requirements, I don't see a problem. Why do you ask?"

But I'd already talked way too much. I needed to be cool, take this one step at a time. Not get any more excited. Yet.

"Just wondering," I said.

I'd hoped Milo would be waiting when I got back outside. He wasn't, so I ran to Mom and Dad, who were standing at the refreshments table with Sandy Mathias, drinking hot cider. I could see the curls of steam rising from their cups. "I think I may have just had my interview to go here!" I said, handing Dad the application. "With this lady, Meg, who turned out to be dean of students."

I thought I saw a twinkle in Sandy's eyes. "You talked to Dr. Dunham?"

Mom and Dad looked somewhat surprised. But also, not.

"The question is what do I do till then?" I said. "I mean, next year is so far away."

"Whoa! Slow down," Dad said. "From what Sandy's been telling us, it's not easy getting in here."

"I know," I said. "But I don't think I'll have a problem."

I might not even need another interview. Should I tell them that?

"Well, that's great, but don't forget, kiddo, you still have to apply." Dad pretended to be weighing the application packet. "This feels like a lot of forms and essays. And I'm sure they'll need recommendations too, so you'll have to work extra-hard and get good grades. That should keep you busy. And there's camp next summer, if you want. I promise," he said with a glance at Mom. "The year will fly by."

"That's not what I meant," I said.

"And you can always go back to those projects you started," Mom said. "I mean, what ever happened to your diabetes research, and your plants, and working with Milo and Dimitri from camp, and Mr. Horton?"

"I know." I nodded. "I want to. Meg . . . Dr. Dunham . . . wants me to."

Here was my chance. My heart lollopped.

"What if I did all those things you just said, but not at . . ."

I looked at Sandy for support. But before I'd even said the word *school,* Dad got the old *Oh, no not again!* look in his eyes.

257

"I know!" I said. "You're school people. You like to do things the regular, not weird, not scary way. But what if I could be a"—I knew enough not to say homeschool, or unschool—"not-school person? In a not-weird, non-loose way? What if I signed a contract, like what Milo did, with Freedoms on one side of the list and Responsibilities on the other? What if we talked to everyone we could think of, including Meg, to come up with a plan for the rest of the year? We could go back and ask her now. Or I could work with Preston, right, Sandy? He'll have plenty of time without Milo around. Mom, remember what he said about giving me the gift of the year of freedom? And it's not even a whole year now. It's only . . ."—I counted on my fingers—"eight more months."

Mom and Dad just looked at each other. They looked sad.

CHAPTER 29

The sunset was turning the sky all violet and orange when I met Milo by the rock at Alvin's field. The wind was so fierce here at the top of the hill that the patchwork pajamas flapped against his legs, and my hair whipped into my eyes. I tucked it inside my jacket collar and hugged my arms around myself. I'd have hugged him, but I didn't dare. Not with his new violin case in his hand.

"So how is it?" I asked. He'd sounded totally excited when he'd called to apologize for never making it to the school.

"Really amazing. Wanna hear? It's kind of too cold for my hands, but . . ." His eyes were shining. "And you liked New Directions! I knew it!"

He set the case down on the rock and opened the lid.

As he got out the bow and tightened it, I told him more about the Meg interview.

"But they still won't let me leave MVB," I said.

"And are you really upset? Sorry. Dumb question." He lifted out the violin for me to see. "It's a redder brown than mine. Pretty, huh?"

I nodded. It was almost the same chestnutty color as his hair.

"So what are you gonna do?"

"Besides grin and bear it? Or not grin and not bear it? I don't know." I shrugged. "Get some extremely contagious and long-lasting but painless disease?"

"That violinists can't catch?"

"Exactly."

"Or you can do stuff with me," he said. "As soon as the competition's over and I'm at school. Maybe it won't be so bad." He tucked the violin under his chin. "Guess how much it's worth."

"A million dollars?"

"Not quite, but a lot. So's the bow."

"Will it help you win?"

"I don't know. See what you think." He climbed up on the rock, and after quickly tuning, began to play something with a melody so high and haunting, I could feel the sweetness of it in my throat.

"If that's the Mendelssohn, you'll win," I said when he finished. "You'll definitely win. No question."

He shivered. "If my hands don't fall off." He jumped down off the rock and put the violin back in its case. "Are you too cold?"

"Yes!" I said.

"Wanna go?"

"No." A full moon was starting to come up behind the hills. "It's too nice here."

"I know." He moved closer and wiggled his hands into the back pockets of my jeans. "Mmm. This helps."

"Yeah." I put my hands in his back pockets. "It does." I was shivering now too, but not from the cold.

"So are you gonna ever tell me I was right?" he said into my hair.

"About making me go see New Directions?"

He pressed closer. "Uh-huh."

"I still hate the name," I said. "But yeah. You were really right."

I eased my hands from his pockets and put my arms around his neck and kissed him. Hard. The shivering had changed to trembling. An insanely happy, buzzy, humming, inside trembling that made me babble: "You know what would make everything really perfect? If moonshine was warm. And we heard a coyote. Did you know you can get a coyote ringtone for your phone? Too bad we don't have it now, or we could use it to call one and with the full moon, maybe it would answer and . . . I love you!" The words blurted out so suddenly. I could feel my face getting hot. I couldn't see his face. But maybe that was good.

He stepped away from me, put his hand up to his mouth like a phone, and in an English accent, said, "Hello, is this Mr. Coyote? Milo, here. Or . . . Hey, who needs a phone!" He tipped back his head and howled. "Arooooooooooooooo!"

He had to have heard me say it. I felt like everyone in town had heard me. A dull hurt was filling up my chest, but I punched his arm.

"That's not a coyote," I said. "That's Waffle. A coyote's more like . . ." I did a high-pitched "Yip, yip, yip!"

He threw back his head again and let out a bloodcurdling set of yips with an *aroo* on the end. "Is that better?"

"You sound more like an ambulance than a coyote."

"How's this, then?"

"It's okay, Milo," I said. "You can stop howling."

"Okay." He pried my arms apart, fitted his hands inside my jacket and slipped them up under my shirt. I flinched as his icy fingers touched my skin, but only for an instant. He moved his mouth close to my ear. "Hey," he whispered. "You know I love you."

30

I went straight to my room when I got home, to get into bed and dream about seeing him at the field again tomorrow night. But I could hear Mom and Dad through the floor, talking. And I'm like Waffle when I hear my name. Mom's voice was getting kind of loud. It sounded like they were arguing about New Directions. I could understand them not letting me leave school right now, but . . .

No, I couldn't!

I put in my earbuds, got under the covers, and tried to let the music sweep away everything but Milo. *You know I love you.* His voice so matter-of-fact, even as he whispered it. I did know. And even without knowing it, I'd known I loved him, since . . . maybe since that first "Yaaaaaaaahhhhhh!" out on the field.

But remembering that scream just reminded me why I was out walking the road that night.

They still don't get it! They're never gonna get it! I'm right back where I started. I could already hear myself saying it to Dr. Gordon Monday. *And what if New Directions won't take me? What if I get rejected? I mean, it's not like they'll care. I mean, it'll make their life a whole lot easier. But what'll I do? Go to . . .*

Why was he smiling? Even the Dr. Gordon in my head had an infuriating smile. I could already hear his answer too: *Forget them. Never mind next year. What are you gonna do with the rest of this year?*

I took out the earbuds, got out of bed, and texted Francesca.

📱 r u doing anything 2moro?
no. y? she answered instantly.
wd u want to maybe work on the article? o and btw,
i have big news!!!!!

As soon as her mom's car pulled up the next morning, I ran out to meet her.

"So I found a school!" I said. "Milo was so right! I loved it!"

"I knew it." She hugged me. "I knew it before you went. I totally knew it!"

Her mouth was smiling, but her eyes didn't seem too happy.

"It's not till next year," I assured her. "Which sucks, except for not leaving you."

I told her how I'd typed up my project notes last night, and printed out the picture of Bucky/Buckerina, and checked just now to see if my garlic mustard plants were really and truly dead. Which, of course, they were. "But we can write about what the experiment was going to be," I said. "And explain that in the spring—"

"I didn't know your mom had a beauty salon," she said. She was looking at the sign on the side of the garage: A CUT ABOVE, and a giant pair of scissors

My stomach dropped. It was my one remaining giant secret.

Why does it have to be a secret anymore? part of me prodded. *Just tell her.* The other part was like, *If she didn't even know the salon existed, why tell her anything?*

"She does," I said. The blood was roaring in my ears.

"That's so cool," she said. "My mom would give anything to work at home."

"And when you thought I was in New Haven doing Zen archery? And generally unschooling?" If I looked at her, I'd never keep going. "I was actually up there with her. All day every day. I had a desk behind the hair dryers. And a Daily Instructional Matrix. Which is why I wouldn't let you come over here. Because I didn't want you to see what I was really doing. Or not doing."

"Gotcha." She stood there, hands jammed in her pockets, biting her lip, frowning.

My ears were totally roaring now. "So now you hate me for lying to you?"

"Hate you? Why would I hate you?" She kicked at the gravel in the path. "I mean, you still did it."

"Did what, besides lied?"

She tilted her head and looked at me like I was stupid. "What you wanted to. I haven't even written the article."

"Yeah, that's why you're here," I said.

"Not that one. The 'No More Games' one." She smoothed out the gravel she'd kicked up. "The one about me quitting playing."

"I didn't think you were seriously doing that," I said.

"Exactly," she said.

Duh. She didn't care a bit about my secret. She was just upset about herself. The relief of it made me feel like dancing.

"So then we'll do it now. We'll use Mom's computer. And you'll get to see where the finest school secretaries go for their coiffures." I fished the key from inside the lantern and we went up. The apple-y sweet smell of hair products hit us as I opened the door. "Not that Pinchbeck was ever here when I was," I said. "Thank goodness! But if she was"—I went over to the line of dryers, sat in the first chair, and ducked my head inside one of the giant, heavy hoods—"she'd have been right here. And I'd have turned it on for her, and brought her a *Woman's Day* or whatever, and checked her rollers. That's what I did when I wasn't doing my Dreaded DIM. Which I can show you too, if you want. But the good thing about being up here"—why had it taken me till now to realize there was something good about it?— "was Mr. Horton. If Mom didn't make me do his feet, I'd have never met him. Or seen the beaver, or heard of invasive plants. Plus, in case you ever need your feet washed, I do a killer foot wash."

I'd thought Francesca would have said something by now. She was still over by the door, still biting her lip.

266

I raised the hair dryer hood so I could get out of it, went over and took her arm, and led her to the computer.

"Trust me. You'll feel so good," I said. "I mean, you already have the title. 'Why Francesca Thinks School Is a Load of—'"

"I can't," she said. "I'm not brave like you."

"Brave? Excuse me? So brave I pretended the tree house got struck by lightning to keep you from coming over? So brave I—"

"You are," she said. "You know you are. I was serious when I said I needed the Homeschool Liberation League."

"I needed it too," I said. "I still need it. Why do you think I made it up?"

"I'll write it," she said. "Just not now, okay?"

"Then how 'bout after your spa pedicure?" It popped out without my planning. "Minus the pedicure part, which I don't know how to do. But we can do the aromatherapy foot soak."

Her face unfurrowed. "Deal." She climbed onto the pedicure chair and pulled her shoes off. "And I can do our nails. I'm great at nails."

While the basin filled, I thumbed through the selection of packets. "Okay, so Lavender Mist washes away anxiety." There were three envelopes of lavender. I sprinkled in all of them. "And Tea Tree's stimulating and energizing. Also antibacterial, in case your feet are gross."

"They're pretty gross," she said.

They weren't, of course. They were as perfect as the rest of her. But mine were, so I dumped in a packet of Tea Tree, and then, for the fun of it, some Rosemary and Thyme, and then some Petal, to balance out the sort of Italian restaurant smell.

"Uh, Katya?" She'd pulled her feet up under her. "The water's looking a little toxic here." It had turned a prune-juicey purplish brown and was bubbling ferociously. "Are you supposed to put all those . . . ?"

"Probably not," I said. "But it smells like it's gotta be really good for you. And I'm brave, right? Scootch over." I stepped out of my Birks, climbed up, and squeezed in next to her. She had to unfold her legs to make room for me. "Hold on!" I'd also forgotten to check the temp. I leaned over and felt it. "Perfect. You can put your feet in. Now for the Scratchomatic."

I set the Magic Fingers to High Knead. The chair shuddered into action, then gave me such a poke in the ribs I let out a yelp.

She laughed. "Why is it," she said as I quickly turned it down, "that whenever we get together we do something ridiculous? I never do ridiculous things with anyone but you."

"Maybe next we should try Zen archery," I said.

"What is Zen archery, anyway?"

I shrugged. "No clue. I thought you knew. And this isn't ridiculous, by the way. It's great."

"I agree," she said.

We wriggled around till the Magic Fingers could get to both our backs, and let the hot water burble around our ankles.

We'd barely gotten to the computer when her sister came

to pick her up. But we had extremely clean feet and Gladi-ola toenails. And a start on the first paragraph. I'd thought of a totally kick-ass first line. And it turned out her sister wasn't in a rush, so Francesca did her nails too.

"We'll write the rest next time," she said as I locked up the salon. "I swear. Really. But this was so much fun."

I nodded. "Fun is good," I said.

Dad and Mom were cleaning up from lunch when I came in. The kitchen smelled like toast and bacon. There was a tomato on the counter. BLTs. My favorite.

"Did you save me any bacon?" I asked.

"You can take your year," Mom said. "We've decided to stop fighting it."

"You're saying I can leave MVB?"

My throat almost closed from the shock of it. I looked from Mom to Dad to Mom again. They looked like they were serious.

Dad put down his dishcloth. "We may be old-fashioned and traditional. But we're not blind, kiddo." He walked over and put a hand on my shoulder. "The way you looked, run-ning out of that school yesterday, your face hasn't shone like that once since you've been back at MVB."

"Or ever there, the more we thought about it," Mom added. "It's getting kinda hard to keep hearing you tell us you're miserable. Especially since so far, all your crazy schemes or whatever you want to call them—"

"Dreams," Dad said, catching my eye. "She called them dreams."

"—they've all turned out all right. I mean, starting with camp, and then the month at home . . ."

"Yeah," he said, still holding me with his eyes. "You were ahead of us then. And we're just gonna trust you're ahead of us now."

"We've been on the phone all morning with Preston and Sandy," Mom said. "He said he can help us come up with an instructional plan. So we're thinking between them and Dr. Dunham, if she's willing, and maybe your friend Dimitri, a year of freedom might actually be okay."

"Might?" Why did they still look so serious? "Okay?" My mouth felt like it was going to fly off my face, I was smiling so hard. "It'll be way more than okay," I said. "It'll be the best gift I ever had."

31

"Oh dear! It really does look like snow out there."Ms. Pinch-beck frowned as she peered out the salon window. "I'd hate to have to wear a hat tonight, Donna, after you've made my hair look so pretty!" It was the Friday before winter break. Ms. Pinchbeck was getting a blowout for the winter dance. She turned to me. "Are you going to let her do something special to your hair too, Kaity?"

I was on the little pedicure stool, giving Mr. Horton the deluxe foot spa treatment. Generally speaking I wasn't spend-ing much time in the salon these days. But when I was at his house helping him catalog fossils the other day, he'd asked if the Have Ten, Get One Free offer included me.

"You are coming, aren't you?" Ms. Pinchbeck asked. "Just because you're not at school anymore, that's no reason you can't enjoy yourself."

The old me would have bristled and searched for bril-liant retorts. I acknowledged Mr. Horton's wink and said, "You're right, Ms. Pinchbeck. I'll be there."

Early, in fact. Francesca was the head of the dance com-mittee. Milo, Chloe, and I were helping her set up.

I hadn't seen Milo since his trip to Montreal last weekend. He didn't win the competition. He came in second. So he wasn't getting to play the Mendelssohn Concerto with the orchestra. But something almost as good had happened—to me something way more exciting. A famous New York violin teacher heard him play there and wanted to start teaching him. In New York City. So, starting after the holidays, he was going to be taking the train in every Saturday for lessons. And guess who was going with him, to take a botany class at the New York Botanical Garden? And, when the weather got warm, go on foraging walks with the famous Wild Food Forager of Central Park. And maybe a life drawing course— I'd been doing a lot of drawing lately—though I was a little nervous about seeing naked people.

My parents knew none of this yet, but we'd work it out. Same as we'd worked out my finally, for real, forever leaving MVB. And tutoring with Sandy Mathias, who, we discovered, knew more about natural science than Preston. And just like it would work out for next year with New Directions. Or not. Though I thought it would.

The snow started even before my toes were dry. By the time Grandpa and Cookie arrived for dinner, it was coming down hard. Mom kept checking out the window. We were supposed to be picking up Milo and Chloe.

"Better let me take them in the Subaru," Grandpa said as we ate our chicken. Unlike the night of the dance, this time I remembered to give Cookie's garlic bread a pass. "It's got the all-wheel drive."

"We've got four-wheel drive, Pop," Mom said. "It'll be fine."

"He just wants to get a look at the boyfriend." Cookie smiled across the table at me. "I hear he's adorable."

"And you've met the parents?" Grandpa asked Dad.

"Oh, yes," Dad said. "We like the parents."

Mom pinned the cluster of bittersweet berries in my hair while Dad went to warm up the car. "Stand still!" she said. "And let me give you just a touch more blush."

"She don't need blush," Grandpa called from the sofa. "She's already a killer diller."

"I've got some nice Estée Lauder cologne in my bag," Cookie said. "Want me to give you a spritz?"

I started to say no, but they were both beaming. "Sure," I said.

I'd also thought about not putting an invasive alien vine in my hair, and not letting Mom do my hair in these loose curls. I'd thought about not dressing up either, as a statement of being free. But then I thought, why do I need a statement? So there I was in the shimmery black tee I'd borrowed from Jessie (we weren't best friends anymore, but I still hung out with her and Alyssa every now and then, and they kept me up to date on the news at school), with my sprig of red berries, and Francesca's gorgeous black ballet flats in my backpack so they wouldn't get ruined in the snow.

"Look at you!" Sandy exclaimed when I ran in to get Milo. "What a shame those snowflakes have to melt. They look so magical in your hair."

273

"Yeah, all you need is a few leaves and sticks," Milo said. But he thought I looked good. I could tell.

"You look lovely too, Chloe," Preston said.

I nodded. She had on her same skinny black jeans and black cardigan and black hat, but she'd pinned a large rhinestone starfish on the hat tonight, and put glitter on her eyelids.

"And you, Milo," Preston said, "look excellent!"

"It's Dad's sweater," Milo said with the old eyebrow raise. "That's why he approves." But he seemed easier with his dad than I'd ever seen him.

"And just remember, son," Preston said. "Nobody else knows what they're doing on the dance floor either. They just all stand there in a crowd and wiggle. And they'll be too busy thinking about how they look to be paying attention to you. So just wave your arms and shake your hips—"

"No! Please!" Chloe pulled her hat over her eyes as Preston raised his arms. "Do not demonstrate, Dad! You'll embarrass all of us." She turned to Milo. "And you're not bringing a book this time, right? Speaking of embarrassing."

"You really do look great," he whispered in my ear as soon as we were in the car. Chloe had slid into the front seat with my dad so we could have the backseat to ourselves. "You smell nice too." I took his hand. The streetlights filtering through the snow made everything all soft and otherworldly.

Francesca and her crew had even managed to make the

274

funky, smelly old gym look almost romantic, with a zillion white icicle lights twinkling from the ceiling and pine garlands studded with colored lights draping the windows and doors.

"I didn't want any of that corny, like, 'Frosty the Snowman' stuff this year," she said, looking totally un-Francesca-like in cream Converse high-tops and a jacket she'd found at the consignment shop, and a red bandanna. "Come check out the food!"

Mr. Westenburg already was. "Mmm, that looks scrumptious!" he said, picking up a cupcake. "I think I'll just see if it tastes as good as it looks."

He was wearing a Santa hat.

Ms. Pinchbeck, coming up behind him, had on red and green felt antlers.

"The decorations are just lovely, Francesca," she said. "But where's the blow-up Frosty? I miss Frosty."

"I don't know," I said. "But at least we won't miss Rudolph."

Francesca kicked me. Milo stifled a laugh. But Ms. Pinchbeck smiled gamely.

"Don't tell your mom. She'll kill me for messing up my hair."

"Ha, ha, ha!" Mr. Westenburg laughed that super hearty laugh of his. "That's the advantage of not having any. No hat head. So how's it working out for you this time, Kaitlyn?"

"Good," I said. "Really good. And it's good to be back tonight."

The others were all looking at me like, *Liar!* But I wasn't lying. The room was filling up with kids I wanted to say hi to. And I couldn't believe I'd been so scared of Westenburg before. Or wasted time hating him, when all he was was a blowhard in a Santa hat.

Mr. Z. edged between us to grab a cupcake. "Hey, you guys wrote a fantastic article!" he said as Mr. Westenburg and Ms. Pinchbeck moved down the table toward the punch. "I love all the stuff about the beaver and his nose valves. But you might want to consider toning down the end just a tad, Francesca."

"End?" I looked at her. "You didn't tell me you finished!"

"Blame me," Mr. Z. said. "I told her if she got me a draft before the break, we could run it in the first January issue."

"I took out the word *stupefied*," she told him.

"Oh, wow. But you stuck on the whole school-sucks-and-here's-why thing? You actually did it?"

"Uh-uh!" She looked ridiculously pleased with herself. "It's still about you. And the science projects. I just added a couple little paragraphs about the Homeschool Liberation League."

"You what?" I said. "Excuse me?"

But then the DJ started testing his equipment, and Jess and Alyssa arrived with the Munson twins, whom they were both dating now, and we had to defend the cupcakes from a swarm of sixth-grade boys. So it was a while before I could ask her again.

"You wrote about the Homeschool Liberation League?"

"I did!" she said, looking even more pleased. "And I don't care if it is over the top. It's all true. Kids walking around in their rut need to know things like the Homeschool Liberation League exist."

"Except it doesn't," I said.

"Who says?" she said. "I'm in it. You made me an honorary member. And you guys are in it. Plus, I thought the article needed something you know, 'thus-in-conclusion'-like and inspirational."

I made an *Uh-oh!* face at Milo. "And you said what, exactly?" The music had just started, so I had to shout. The dance was on!

"Here!" She reached under the refreshment table for her backpack and dug around in it till she found a sheet of paper. "Just read the end."

Milo crowded in and read over my shoulder with me.

> You may not have seen kids walking around in Homeschool Liberation League hats or T-shirts. You might have trouble finding their website. They don't have one. But that doesn't make the Homeschool Liberation League any less real. The Homeschool Liberation League is a state of mind.
>
> The Homeschool Liberation League isn't about the homeschooling so much as about the liberation. Just because most

people do something the standard, regular, official way, that doesn't mean it's the
only way. The Homeschool Liberation
League is about being where you need to
be, wherever that is, school or not school,
to be who you know you are. And, if you
can't be where you need to be, it's about
doing whatever it takes, wherever you are,
so that your curiosity and imagination
stay alive and your mind can breathe.

"What?" she demanded as Milo's eyebrow shot up.

"Not to hurt your feelings, Francesca, but noses breathe,"
he shouted back. "Not minds."

"Fine," she said. "It's a draft. I'll change it. But you know
as well as I do, if your mind can't breathe, you might as well
be dead. And if your heart is squashed . . ."

"Aiiiii!" I groaned. "Where's my violin?" I waved to Mr.
Z. "Hey, Mr. Z., call the corniness police!"

She punched me. "Yeah, but it's all true, right? Come
on, you're smiling, Katya! You agree. You like it. You love it!
Admit it!"

"Okay, I do," I yelled. I did. But then, happy as I was, I'd
have agreed with almost anything. "I just want to know one
thing. Do we have to be so serious?"

"Yeah, this is a dance!" Milo shouted. "She came here to
dance. With me."

He headed for the dance floor.

"Hey! Where you going? Wait up!" I grabbed his arm and tried out my new eyebrow raise. "You can dance?"

"Yeah," he said, raising his eyebrow right back at me. "Can you?"

Then he put both hands on my waist, steered me through the crowd, and when we found an open spot, he pulled me close. Then—never mind that it was a fast song; who cared if it was a fast song—he tightened his arms around me, and we danced.